THE
Snow Pony

THE
Snow Pony

ALISON LESTER

Houghton Mifflin Company Boston 2006

Walter Lorraine Books

Acknowledgments
Many thanks to Helen Packer, Sue van der Heide,
and Sue Indian for the photographs, Dusty for the name,
and everyone who shared their stories with me.

Walter Lorraine *wx* Books

www.houghtonmifflinbooks.com

Library of Congress Cataloging-in-Publication Data
Lester, Alison.
  The Snow Pony / by Alison Lester.
    p. cm.
Summary: Prolonged drought has strained Dusty's ranching family
to the breaking point, but she finds consolation with her wild and
beautiful horse.
  ISBN 0-618-25404-8
  [1. Ponies—Fiction. 2. Wild horses—Fiction. 3. Ranching—Fiction.
4. Rescue—Fiction. 5. Australia—Fiction.] I. Title.
  PZ7.L56284 Sn 2003
  [Fic]—dc21
                                                    2002013388

HC ISBN-13: 978-0-618-25404-0

PA ISBN-13: 978-0-618-77125-7
PA ISBN-10: 0-618-77125-5

Printed in the United States of America
VB 10 9 8 7 6 5 4 3

FOR MUM

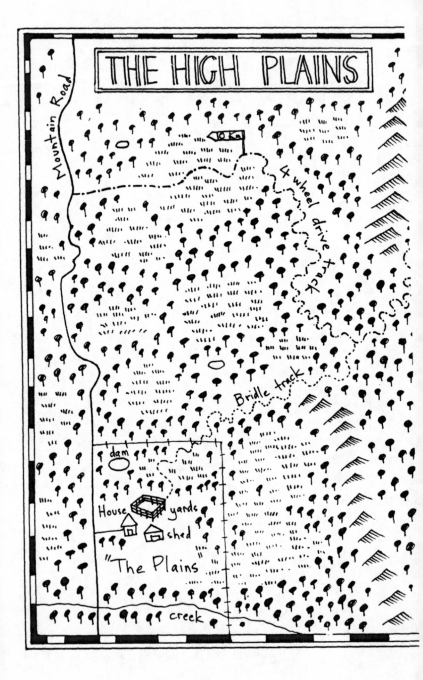

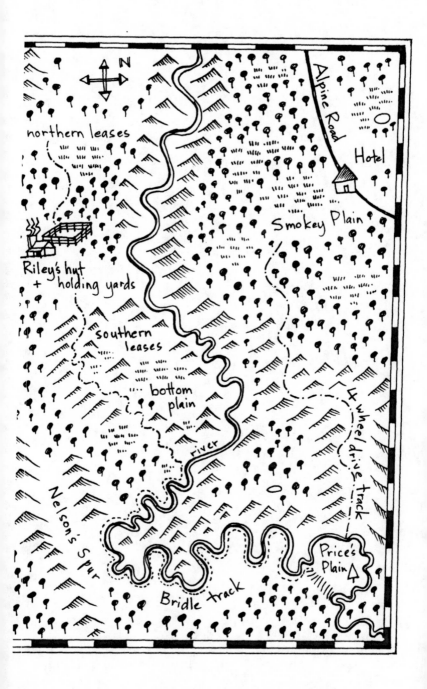

TABLE OF CONTENTS

THE
Snow Pony

PART ONE

1

The Plains

Dusty was eleven when they found the Snow Pony. She and her father had driven up to the high plains at the start of spring, skidding through the mud and melting snow, to check their house up there for winter storm damage. She always looked forward to that first visit after the road opened, when the snow-covered plains looked clean and uninhabited.

Back then, Dusty loved being with her dad, just her and him. It was good with Mum and Stewie around as well, but when it was just the two of them, Dusty felt as if they were a team, ready for anything. She felt there was nothing Jack couldn't handle. When she was tiny he had seemed so powerful she'd thought for a while that he must be boss of the whole country—the prime minister or even king of Australia—and that nobody was telling her in case she got a swollen head. Jack Riley always won, always beat his opponent—the misbehaving horse, the cranky bullock, the headstrong dog, the truck that wouldn't start—and she was his sidekick, his right-hand man. He didn't say it to her, but she'd heard him telling other cattlemen, at sales and musters: "Yeah, this is Dusty. She's my right-hand man."

Sometimes she wondered how Stewie, her little brother, felt about it. Jack didn't spend nearly as much time with him, and Dusty knew that people thought it was strange that she worked outside with her dad while Stewie stayed inside drawing space monsters and making mobiles and tagging along after Mum. Stewie just didn't like the farm work very much. He had nearly died when he was a baby, and Jack said that Rita had been over-protective of him ever since.

∾

The Rileys were cattle farmers, and had been for four generations. Dusty and Stewie were the fifth. The Willows, where Dusty and her family lived, was their home property, but it was their other land, fifty kilometres away, high above the snowline in the mountains, that made the Rileys' farm so special. They called it The Plains, because of the wide expanses of alpine grassland up there. At the start of every summer they took three days to walk the cows and their little calves up to The Plains. The cattle stayed there until Easter, growing strong on the lush clover that grew under the twisted snow gums, while the paddocks below at The Willows turned brown in the blistering summer sun.

Each year in autumn, before snow came to The Plains, the Rileys would muster their herd of three hundred Hereford cows and calves and drive them back down the mountain to The Willows. The calves were about ten months old by then, ready to be weaned and sold at the Banjo calf sales. Calves from the high country had a reputation for growing into fine bullocks, so cattle buyers came from all over eastern Australia to bid for them.

When there had been good rains over summer, and plenty of grass to fatten the calves, prices were high, but in times of drought the cheque from the calf sales was pitiful.

The Plains was so remote and the landscape so different from anywhere else that going there was like going to another country, and Dusty and Stewie were always nagging their parents to spend a whole winter there. "Go on, Mum," Dusty would plead, her dark eyes dancing just at the thought of it. "It'd be fantastic. Stew and I could do correspondence school, and you and Dad could make whips and bridles and sell them when we came back down . . . When the weather was good we could ski out to Nelson's Spur and look for brumbies. We might even see a deer! We could have skiing races, just the four of us."

The last time they had talked about it, at Christmas, Rita went along with the game for a while, pulling Dusty's head on to her lap and ruffling her glossy black hair. "You and Stewie would miss the TV too much," she teased. "You couldn't live without TV."

They talked about what they'd miss, the supplies they'd take, how to grow bean shoots in a jar, for fresh greens, and then both their voices trailed away and they sat together in silence, not saying but thinking that it wouldn't really be any fun at all. In the old days, before the drought, it would have worked, but now that Dad was always tense and angry the thought of being locked up with him for the whole winter was a nightmare.

∾

But back when Dusty and Jack went up to The Plains that

3

spring, two and a half years ago, things hadn't yet turned bad. They arrived on a grey evening without a breath of wind. The homestead stood like a lonely doll's house among the snow gums. The carpet of white around the house was dotted with holes where sticks and leaves had started to fall through the melting snow.

Dusty slammed the door of the truck. "Throw us the key Dad, and I'll . . ."

A sudden crashing from the shed tore the silence apart. Two horses charged past the house in a panic of mud, snow, and flying mane.

"What the . . . ?" Jack looked at Dusty and raised his eyebrows. "Where did *they* come from?"

Together they walked to the shed. The gate across the front was open and bent.

"Do you think they did that on purpose, Dad? Broke in so they could get to the hay? I didn't think horses were that clever."

Jack shook his head. "They must have been starving. Must have been up here at the start of winter then couldn't get down to the lower country through the snow. The brumbies always shelter on the north side over winter, where the snow's not so deep and it's warmer. Look at the mess. Been camped in here a long time."

It looked more like they'd been wrestling inside the shed, thought Dusty. The hay was normally stacked neatly at the back, but now there were broken bales all over the place. The earth floor was a stinking mess of rotten hay and manure.

"Mmmnn. I hope you're feeling strong, mate. We'll have to clean that up tomorrow." Jack turned and shaded his eyes to look across the home paddock. The horses stood in the far corner, looking nervously back to the shed. "Well, they don't seem to want to clear out," he said. "You'd think they'd have disappeared by now."

Dusty squinted to see them better. A pinto and a dun— no, a grey. "Maybe they haven't got anywhere else to go. Maybe they want to stay with us." Suddenly she grabbed her father's arm. "Maybe one of them can be a pony for me! A wild horse, like the Silver Brumby!"

Jack smiled ruefully and shook his head. "You're a dreamer. No, even if you could catch them, I doubt you'd ever tame that grey. She looked as wild as the wind."

༄

Dusty was dreaming. A laughing polar bear was rolling her through the snow, pushing her over and over . . .

"Dusty! Wake up!"

She opened her eyes. Her father was kneeling beside her swag.

"Dad! I thought you were a polar bear . . ."

"Ssshhh!" He put his finger in front of his lips. "Keep quiet!"

Dusty looked around the lounge room. After dinner last night they had rolled out their swags and slept in front of the fire. The bedrooms were always freezing, and Dusty felt a bit spooky without Stewie in the other bed.

"Why are the dogs inside?"

Digger and Spike were never allowed in the house, but now they were basking in the glow of the fire, looking very smug.

"I didn't want them to frighten away the brumbies, if they came back. And they have."

Dusty tiptoed to the window and peered through a rip in the blind. The yard was flooded with moonlight, and moving silently through it were the horses, pale blue and ghostly. The pinto was a typical brumby, with a big box-shaped head and a runty body that looked as if it were made of spare parts from other horses. But the grey was beautiful. Her shaggy winter coat and poor condition couldn't hide her graceful lines.

"She's a beauty, isn't she?" Jack whispered. "And she's not fully grown yet. She's only a baby."

The grey mare was closer to the house than the pinto, and Dusty could see the tension in her finely boned head. Her mane and tail were much darker than her coat; almost black. At first Dusty thought the horse had patches of snow on her rump, but now she could see that they were actually white dots scattered over her grey coat, like a patterned blanket.

The horses went into the shed and Dusty imagined herself scampering over the snow, shutting the gate behind them, catching them, and then taming the snowy one for herself, but she knew it was a fantasy. These were wild horses. They'd have to be trapped in the main yards, with high solid fences that they couldn't jump. The moon was behind the shed, so she couldn't see in—it was as if the horses disappeared into a black hole. A muffled thump came from inside and Dusty started to giggle as she imagined the horses wrestling amongst the hay bales.

"What are you laughing at?" Jack said, but suddenly Digger was at the window, barking hysterically. The snowy brumby came flying out of the shed and Dusty had never seen anything move so fast or so lightly. Her hooves

6

barely touched the ground, and she was gone before the pinto was even past the gate. As the mare flashed past the window, Dusty could see an open wound on her shoulder; an ugly tear ringed with a ragged crust of dried blood and pus. Jack saw it, too.

"She's had dingoes after her. No wonder she's scared of dogs." He turned to Dusty. "What a horse! Maybe we should have a go at catching her. I've known blokes ride brumbies they've caught in the bush and some of them were pretty smart horses, too, but I wouldn't call them kids' ponies."

Dusty huffed. Her father knew she could handle a difficult horse. "I haven't been riding Shetland ponies all my life."

Jack laughed. "I know. I know you're a good rider, but this would be something else again. It would make those young thoroughbreds you help your mother with seem like donkeys. Still, we'll give it a go. If they hang around, we might try and catch her when we come up to muster next autumn. She'll have filled out a bit by then. If she'll let herself be gentled and broken in, she might turn out all right. You never know, maybe she *will* be your pony."

∞

Dusty and Jack slept. The old brown blinds kept out the moonlight, and in the darkened house Digger listened with pricked ears, but didn't bark again. The horses moved like wraiths back across the snowy yard and fed in the shed, and not a sound disturbed the night.

7

2

The Willows

Dusty lived a long way from everywhere. It took four hours to drive from the city to Bankstown, their nearest big town, then another hour to Banjo, their little town, then another fifteen minutes out to The Willows. The country became more and more hilly as you got close to their farm, and when Dusty imagined looking back from outer space she pictured them tucked away in one of a thousand little wrinkles on the earth's surface.

The farm was at the end of Crystal Creek Road, a dipping single lane of gravel that meandered down a wide valley ringed with folding hills.

Her great-grandparents had built their house on the far side of the creek, and it always felt special to Dusty that you had to go over a bridge to get home. It was like being in a castle with a moat and drawbridge. The bridge was made of loosely bolted planks and it clanked and rattled like a grumpy old man every time a car crossed over.

If you turned right after the bridge you came to the stockyards and sheds. Left brought you to the house, almost hidden by an overgrown garden. The creek was so close that Dusty could hear the water gurgling as she lay in bed at night. The house was a rambling weatherboard building with a corrugated iron roof and four brick chimneys. A concrete path led you through the towering box hedge, past the rotary clothesline and under the date palm that Great Grandma had planted. Once, when Dusty was a tiny girl, she had run over Tabby's tail with her trike, as the cat lay sunning herself on the path. The crooked crack in the path always reminded her of the matching kink in her old cat's tail.

Everyone used the back door. There wasn't even a path to the front door; you only went out there on summer evenings to sit on the verandah and watch the light fading over the creek, or to hide, curled-up with a book, when there were jobs to be done. The back porch had been closed-in years ago and it was always a mess; the transition zone between the farm and the house. Here you took off your boots and your muddy trousers, hung up your coat, washed in the laundry trough, and *then* came into the house. The first room was the kitchen and it was the hub of the house—the nerve centre, Jack used to call it. Everything happened here: homework, cooking, sewing, and planning.

The colours of the kitchen took you by surprise when you first walked in, because the cupboard doors were all painted different colours: red, yellow, blue, and green. Dusty's grandmother had seen the look in a magazine in the 1950s, and painted it herself. Since then, no one had had the heart to change it. "Anyway," said Rita, "if we wait long enough it'll come back into fashion."

The rest of the house was much grander than the kitchen. A wide passage led to the glass-panelled front door with a leadlight window of gum leaves and blossoms above it. The lounge room was on one side at the front, and Stewie and Dusty's bedroom was on the other, with its own fireplace. Dusty sometimes thought about moving into the spare room and having a room of her own, but Stewie was scared of the dark, and she'd miss going to sleep with the flickering fire and the sound of the creek.

∾

Dusty knew every gully and every stand of trees on their farm. She knew it so well that she felt part of the land. She loved the smell of the earth in summer—warm and woody—a combination of dirt, twigs, gumnuts, and grass seeds. She even liked the smell of the cattleyards: dust in summer, mud in winter, with creosote from the oiled rails, the chemical odour of the drenches and dips they used to treat the cattle, the sweat, blood, and—always—cow manure.

She and her dad worked well together in the yards. When they were selecting cattle from a mob they worked on foot, each holding a length of lightweight black poly-pipe to direct the cattle. Jack would pick out cattle in the yard and call out directions to Dusty, on sentry duty at the gate, "Okay, let in this old baldy cow with the bent horn. Block the next two. We want this roan one . . . and the one after her . . . not this one with the patch on her eye." And all the time he'd be moving through the yard, pushing cattle one way or another with a tap of his plastic cane.

Stewie sometimes hung around the cattleyards when they were working, but he didn't join in. "You just keep well out the way!" yelled Jack. Once, Stewie had been day-dreaming and let a mob of cows escape through the gate he was meant to be guarding. They'd got into the vegetable patch and trampled all that summer's supply of lettuce.

∾

Dusty's life was the farm. She loved the horses, the cattle, the dogs, the cats, and talked to them all the time. Her best friend, Sally, thought she was crazy when she waved to the horses. "They can't wave back, you know, Dusty. They haven't got arms." Sally could always make Dusty laugh. She was tiny and fair with thick glasses that made her look slightly cross-eyed. Her parents ran Hillside Holidays, where people from the city came to fish and hike and eat the gourmet meals that Sally's mother cooked. Their property was in the same valley, but closer to town, so Sally and Dusty had travelled to school together ever since preps. They were the only two girls in that year, so it was a good thing they got on so well.

"Opposites must attract," Dusty overheard Sally's mum saying once to Rita, "because you couldn't get two more different kids. Sal's away with the fairies most of the time, reading, painting, dreaming, making lists." She laughed. "I've never known anyone to make lists like her. Then you've got Dusty, so practical and capable and even physically so different. She looks like she's been carved from a bit of red gum, she's so muscular and strong."

The truth was that even though Dusty loved the horse and cattle work and proving she was as capable as an adult, she relished those playful times with Sally when she could just be a kid. When Sally stayed at The Willows she rode alongside Dusty on Jack's old grey gelding, and stock work was always fun then. Jack had bellowed at her once, when she chased some cows in the wrong direction, so she

11

didn't actually do anything now, just tagged along. She was always doing nutty things like drawing on Spook with charcoal, or folding his ears under the browband so he looked like a camel. Dusty wished the farm work could always be such fun, instead of everything having to go like clockwork — with a drama if it didn't — and always having to impress her dad.

"He really blows his top, doesn't he?" Sally grinned after he'd yelled at her. "My dad doesn't care if the cows get in the wrong paddock."

"But your farm isn't a proper farm, Sally." Even though Jack had embarrassed her, Dusty felt she had to stick up for him. "Your cows are just there for the tourists. It really matters on this farm if things aren't right." But even as she said it, Dusty knew that Sally had a point. Jack was way too grumpy and persnickety about his work.

Sally's father was almost the opposite. "No hassles" was his favourite saying, and that's what Jack called him when Sally wasn't around. Milo was tall and lean, with stringy arm muscles, an American accent, and long grey hair that he wore in a ponytail. Once, when he came to pick up Sally, he'd had one of her scrunchies holding his hair in place and Jack had gone on about it for hours after they left. But Dusty loved the way he didn't care about what he looked like. One really hot day at Sally's, Dusty had even seen him wearing an old dress. "Much better air circulation, Dusty. Lets the air flow. Men wear skirts all the time in Fiji."

Milo did all the maintenance at Hillside Holidays, entertained the guests with his guitar, and painted endless pictures of his black-and-white cows. The Rileys' house cow, Spot, had come from Milo's herd. Her mother had died when she was only a few days old, and Milo had given her to Dusty to raise. Dusty had fed her, first from a bottle, then a bucket, and she'd grown into a lovely cow who was so quiet that Dusty and Sally could both sit on her back.

3
The Surprise

Dusty sat outside Christanis' milk bar, sharing Sally's Twisties. She was fizzing like a sherbert bomb. Dad had sent a message with a log truck coming down the mountains that he would be home that afternoon with the cattle. He and his mate, Fred, had gone up to The Plains a week ago to muster and drive the cattle back to The Willows, and Dusty knew he was going to try to catch the Snow Pony. It was six months since Dusty and Jack had surprised the brumbies in the hayshed, and all through the summer holidays and the start of grade six Dusty had never stopped thinking about the beautiful mare.

"Why do you want her so much anyway?" Sally asked, through a mouthful of yellow crumbs. "You've got heaps of horses to ride. You've got too many horses. Nearly every weekend you go to a show with your mum and jump those big scary horses of hers."

"That's just it." Dusty reached for another handful. "None of those horses are mine, or Mum's for that matter. They're all horses she's schooling for other people, getting them started."

Rita had been a champion showjumper when she was

young and although she didn't compete any more, she had a steady business training jumping horses for other people.

She and Jack had met because of her showjumping. She had been heading back to her parents' property, near Melbourne, after doing the East Gippsland shows, when her old truck had spluttered to a stop on the highway. Jack always joked that he stopped because she looked so angry, as if she were about to lay into the old truck with a stick, but it was her wild red corkscrewing hair that really caught his eye. He helped her get the motor started, then insisted on following her to the next town in case she broke down again. He stood talking with her for so long at the service station that her horses started stamping in the truck. By the time she drove away he had her telephone number and address, and the next weekend he drove down from Banjo and took her to the movies.

"Her old boyfriend didn't stand a chance," he used to tell the kids proudly. "I swept her off her feet." Rita said it was just like the song "Twenty-four Hours from Tulsa "—meeting a dark stranger as she drove home. In a way, that was the start of Dusty's name, too, because Dusty Springfield sang that song and Rita loved all her albums.

When her parents talked about that chance meeting, twenty years ago, Dusty thought how lucky it was that they'd met, because they seemed perfect together. Dad was slim, dark, and blue-eyed. Mum was just a bit taller than him, and more solid, with golden freckled skin, crazy hair, and green-grey eyes that you could never tell a lie to.

Dusty scrounged for the last crumbs at the bottom of

15

the Twisties bag. "No, those thoroughbreds are all the same. I want a special horse, and Sal, she's so special. You should have seen her that night."

"Yeah, yeah, you've told me a hundred times. The snow, the moonlight, the spots on her back, the Z-shaped scar." Sally scrunched up the empty Twisties bag and lobbed it into the bin. "In the hole, rock and roll!" She turned to Dusty, laughing, but Dusty hadn't noticed her good shot. She was gazing down the road out of town, lost in thought.

"I just hope that she's still there, so Dad can catch her. He saw her and the pinto when they took the cows up before Christmas, but they might have gone somewhere else over the summer. I might never see her again."

Sally started to laugh at Dusty being such a drama queen, then realised how serious she was and put her arm around her friend. "You'll get her, Dusty, I know. If any-one can catch a wild horse, it's your dad."

The ute came around the corner and Dusty stood up.

"Good luck!" Sally gave her a thumbs up.

"Yeah, see you, Sal." Dusty's stomach was churning.

Stewie was sitting next to Rita; he'd had the day off school again. She threw her bag in the back and slid in beside him.

"We're gunna drive up and meet Dad with the cattle." His face was beaming and he was singing some made-up song under his breath, just loud enough for Dusty to pick up a word here and there. "Up in the mountains lived a horse, horse, horse, da da-da da-da of course, dah dah . . ."

Dusty tried to ignore him. He drove her crazy when he was hyper like this. She leant forward to look at her

16

mother's face, and it was excited, too. They knew something, and Dusty thought she knew too, but she wasn't game to say—just in case it wasn't true. I bet he's got the Snow Pony, she thought. I bet he's caught her.

They drove up the winding gravel road that followed the river into the mountains, and Dusty anticipated the cattle around every bend. Finally, there they were—her father walking in front of the cows, leading his horse, the dogs flitting behind him like red shadows, but no grey brumby. Rita stopped the car and Jack leant in the window to kiss her.

"Good to see you all." He looked at their faces—Rita and Stewie beaming and Dusty disappointed—and couldn't bear to see Dusty so sad. "There's something for you at the back of the mob, mate." He was grinning like a fool.

Dusty screamed. "You got her? Oh, Dad! Is she okay?"

He nodded. "Yep, she's good. I'll tell you later about catching her. But I've got to keep going now, these cows are starting to bank up." The cows were crowding around the car, sniffing curiously. "Fred's leading her off his big horse." He swung into the saddle and called the dogs to heel, then rode down the road so the cows could follow.

It seemed to take forever for the mob to pass, and it felt as though their car was swimming upstream while three hundred cows moved past them. The calves that had gone up to the high plains last spring as babies were returning as cheeky weanlings, and they propped and spooked at the car.

Finally, Fred came around the corner on his big crossbred horse, Chester, feathery fetlocks swishing as each enormous hoof clopped to the ground. The grey brumby trailed alongside him like a waterlogged dinghy being towed by a tugboat. She was haltered and tied to the horn on Fred's roping saddle. Dusty could see by the dried runs of muddy sweat caked on the mare's legs that she had struggled hard, but she was showing no resistance now, just staring warily at the ute. Chester's massive strength had worn her into submission.

"You've got yourself a wild one here, girl." Fred stopped beside them. "A real lively one. She fought like a cat for the first day, especially when the old pinto turned back. He's quiet as a house cow. We thought he was going to follow us all the way home, but he stopped at Bryce's Cutting, where the road drops down to the river. It was like he couldn't bear to leave the plains."

Dusty remembered the box-headed brumby that had been with the Snow Pony the night they first saw her, and how closely they'd stuck together. The mare would miss him. She couldn't see the brumby past Chester's bulk.

"Can I come around that side and have a look at her?"

"Sure." Fred glanced back. "But be careful. She's wild and she moves like lightning."

Dusty edged under the arc of Chester's neck, keeping close to him, ready to duck back if the mare went berserk. "Whoa, girl," she crooned softly. "You've had a hard time, haven't you?"

The Snow Pony was standing close to Chester's hind-quarters, the halter rope hanging in a loop, and she didn't pull back and take up the slack as the girl inched towards her. Dusty caught her smell for the first time, sharper than that of a normal horse.

18

"Take it easy," Fred murmured, sitting very still. "She went off like a rocket every time we touched her. She doesn't mind the other horses, but she hates us."

The Snow Pony wasn't going off, though. She didn't even look fearful as Dusty gently offered her hand to smell. She sniffed it casually and stood in the same relaxed position beside Chester. Dusty moved slowly to her shoulder, her heart racing in case the mare struck out, but she didn't. She stood there like a tired old pony, her ears pricked towards Dusty's voice, and let the girl stroke her neck.

"Well I'll be . . ." Fred said softly. "She must be a ladies' horse."

❧

Fred was right. When they began to handle the Snow Pony it was obvious that she was much more relaxed with Dusty and Rita than Jack, or even Stewie. They worked on her all that winter, teaching her to lead first, picking her feet up, rubbing around her ears and introducing her to things she'd never seen before, like plastic bags and buckets.

Dusty spent all her spare time with the Snow Pony, talking to her in a soft sing-song voice, telling her what had gone on at school that day, her secret thoughts, things she would never tell anyone. She caressed and groomed her until she knew every part of the mare, every whorl of hair, every variation in colour and every scratch and scar.

Rita always had to call Dusty to dinner. She was at the yards with her horse every night, talking, stroking, feeding her, then warming herself against the mare's body as the chilly darkness settled around them. When she did finally come inside and sit at the table she talked endlessly about the Snow Pony: how cute she looked when she pricked her ears, how round her feet were and wasn't it good that they were all black, and did they know that she had fourteen white spots on her back? Finally Rita spoke for the whole family and told her to put a sock in it.

Dusty talked constantly about her horse to Sally, too, and although Sally joked about it, putting her hands over her ears and singing to drown out the horsey words, Dusty's preoccupation with the Snow Pony bored her. Dusty never wanted to play at Sally's any more, and when Sally went to the Rileys' she spent all her time sitting on the fence watching Dusty with her horse. It was torture for Sally to sit still and not make any sudden movements that might startle the Snow Pony, and no matter how hard she tried, she always did something to frighten the mare. Dusty never said anything, but Sally could tell when she was mad because her mouth set in a tight line and she started talking more to the Snow Pony and less to her. After this had happened a couple of times, Sally stopped asking to come over because she knew what it would be like: her getting bored on the fence and Dusty getting grumpy.

Rita thought the Snow Pony would make a good showjumper. There was something about the line of her shoulder and her slight goose rump that suggested she would be. "We won't push it," she told Dusty. "I've seen too many horses ruined by jumping them before they're ready. She's still only a four-year-old. We'll let her fill out a bit more."

But the Snow Pony hadn't been prepared to wait. She lived in the high stockyards for three weeks after Fred led her down from the plains, because Jack was afraid she might crash into a wire fence while she was still wild, or escape and run all the way back to her piebald mate on the plains. Chester's half brother, Captain—Rita's horse—lived in the little creek paddock beside the stockyards and he fell in love with the Snow Pony as soon as he saw her. He was so big he could reach right over the yard fence and rub his teeth back and forward gently on her wither, while she reached up and did the same thing to the side of his neck. When Jack finally decided that she was quiet enough to let into the holding paddock, she was so fond of Captain that nothing would have induced her to run away.

One morning as they drove to school, Dusty noticed that the Snow Pony was in Captain's paddock and assumed her father had put the mare there. When she got home from school that night he asked her why *she'd* done it. Mystified, they caught the Snow Pony and led her back to her paddock, then watched as she galloped across the paddock, whinnying madly to Captain. She looked as wild as she did that first night they saw her. She raced towards the fence and Dusty cried out, "Dad! She's going to crash!" But there was no twanging wire or screams of pain. The Snow Pony flew over the fence like an arrow and propped beside Captain in a swirl of mane.

"How's that?" Dusty turned to her father in excitement but he was shaking his head.

"That's feral. I don't think we'll ever tame this one."

As Dusty got to know the Snow Pony, the horse began to know and trust her in return. At first she always had to be tempted with some oats to be caught, and any sudden movement made her leap as though she'd received a jolt of electricity. It was a slow process teaching an animal, whose only defence was flight, to stay and trust them. Dusty learned just how patient you had to be with a young horse; not to expect too much, not to expect every lesson to be remembered.

"A horse can take a long time to learn something," Jack told her, "but once they've learned it, they never forget. And that goes for bad things as well as good. If you hurt a horse, he'll remember it. Look at old Spook. Since that mongrel farrier, Donahue, lost his temper and beat him, he's always been hard to shoe. He associates having his feet picked up with pain."

Dusty ran her hand softly down the Snow Pony's shoulder. That was never going to happen to her horse.

The short winter days had usually closed to darkness by the time Dusty got home from school, so Jack saved most of the handling sessions for the weekend. They were "breaking her in." A lot of people didn't like to use that term, because it implied that you were breaking the horse's spirit, but Jack reckoned it was fair enough.

"You can love her as much as you like," he told Dusty. "But you've got to be the boss. I've seen too many spoilt horses that have been 'gentled.' Charlie Hicks sent a horse down to some cowboy at Maffra last year and when it came back it was useless. Didn't know a thing. When he rang up to complain, the fella told Charlie the horse would do anything for a carrot." Jack laughed at the memory. "Charlie said to me, 'I'm not walkin' round with a pocket full of bleedin' carrots.' And he's right. The horse is here to serve you. There's things she has to learn, and I'm not going to hurt her, but I will be tough if I have to."

Dusty found out just how tough when they tied the Snow Pony up for the first time. They hadn't expected much resistance after her trip down from the plains, when she'd been tethered to Fred's saddle and tied up at night. But now that she was stronger she fought like a demon. Jack put a big soft cotton halter on her, knotted at the side so she couldn't choke and plaited extra thick behind her ears so it wouldn't bite into her skin when she pulled back.

The tie-up pole stood in the middle of the holding paddock, and it was what Dusty thought of when her mum described someone as being "as lonely as a post in a paddock": a thick wooden pole about three metres high with its base buried so deeply in the ground that it was as solid as rock. The bottom two thirds of it were ringed with tyres, sitting on top of each other, so that even the most crazy horse could only bounce off rubber. When they tethered the Snow Pony, tying her high so she couldn't get her forelegs over the rope, she stood quietly at first. It wasn't until Rita saddled Captain and rode him away that she went crazy. She leapt and plunged and fought the rope so wildly that Dusty was in tears. She seemed determined to cripple herself, bashing into the tyres, snapping her head back, thudding on to her side. Dusty pleaded with her father to do something, but he was unmoved.

"She's going to stay there all day, and if she kills herself, so be it. Believe me, you don't want a horse that won't tie up. She's learning a lot more than just being tied up, too. She's learning about patience and submission, and not calling the shots." He jumped down from the fence where he and Dusty had been sitting. "Come on, come and check the heifers with me. You'll only get upset watching her. She'll be a different horse after this."

Dusty didn't speak to Jack for the rest the day. She hated it when he wouldn't listen, when he insisted on doing things his way. He was good with horses—better than anyone else in the district—she knew that, but the Snow Pony wasn't just any old horse. Dusty knew she had to be taught, but she didn't think she could ever be tamed. Her wild mountain spirit, which Dusty loved, meant she would fight to the death and you had to make allowances for that.

4

The Battle

Dusty sat on the top rail of the stockyards fence, gripping so hard her knuckles were white. She stayed very still so as not to frighten the Snow Pony. Jack was about to ride her for the first time. He'd mouthed the mare and saddled her and driven her in long reins, and now the moment of truth had come when they would see how she'd react to having a rider on her back. Last night, when they'd talked about it, Jack hadn't been optimistic.

"She's done everything I've asked her to, I have to admit. But the minute she doesn't understand something she panics, and it's a blind panic, as though she just switches off."

"Why don't you let me ride her first?" Dusty asked. "She never panics with me."

Jack shook his head and Rita nodded in agreement. "No way," they said together and Dusty knew they meant it.

The Snow Pony stayed still as Jack put his foot into the stirrup. She'd grown taller since that night they first saw her in the moonlight, a year ago, and stood at about fifteen hands, so she wasn't really a pony any more, but her name had stuck. Her new spring coat gleamed like gunmetal and the scatter of dots on her rump looked more like a trick of light than white dapples. The scar on her shoulder stood out in a dark, ragged Z. She was still slight, so the bridle, headstall, stock saddle, breastplate, and crupper seemed too big for her, as though there was hardly any horse beneath all that gear. That was until Jack gently settled his weight on to her back. Then, before Dusty's very eyes, she grew—getting bigger, swelling, until she exploded into a series of leaps and bounds and bucks that jolted Jack around like a rag doll. He stuck like glue, trying to pull her head up and spurring her forward every time she bucked. Finally she was exhausted, "bucked out," and she propped, legs splayed and sides heaving, dripping with sweat. Jack sat on her for a little while, panting himself, then pushed her forward and she walked quietly around the yard.

"That's more like it." He rewarded her with a pat on the neck. "Good girl." But even as he was saying it he was looking at Dusty and shaking his head.

Dusty felt like howling, but she blinked the tears back. It was shocking to see her horse resisting so violently, and she knew she'd never stay on a bronco like that, but she knew in her heart that the Snow Pony wouldn't buck like that with her. Dad thought he knew everything about horses, but he didn't know about this one, she thought bitterly. He was just going to muck her up.

∾

When Dusty got home from school the next day, Jack had ridden the Snow Pony again and had the bruises to prove it.

"She got rid of me all right," Jack said as he limped

26

about the kitchen. "It's a long time since I've been bucked off a horse, but she did it. She pelted me off. I got back on and stayed on, so I reckon I won the fight, but she certainly won that round."

Rita was chopping up vegetables at the sink and Dusty saw her mouth squash up like a chook's bum, the way it always did when she had something difficult to say.

"What is it, Mum?" She waited for it.

Rita kept chopping. She knew how much the horse meant to Dusty.

"I don't think she's going to work out. I know you love her, but I don't think the Snow Pony is ever going to be a suitable horse for you." She looked at Jack for support and he nodded, rubbing his grazed elbow at the same time. "I don't know anyone who has a better way with horses than your father. Horses *like* him, they go well for him. The fact that the mare is resisting him so determinedly probably means that she just can't be ridden. She might just be too wild."

Dusty walked down the passage to her room and flopped on the bed. She *knew* the Snow Pony was a good horse, her parents just couldn't see it. Stewie crept in, looking mysterious, hands tucked up under his pyjama top.

"I got you a happy tablet, Dusty." He smiled and held out a Tim Tam for her. "They eat these in outer space you know. Really." Dusty looked doubtful so he kept going. "It's true. Whenever they get earth-sick, they have a Tim Tam. Cheers 'em up just like that."

"You're an idiot, Stewie." Dusty pulled his hair into spikes with her chocolaty fingers. "But thanks."

"You're not wild, are you?" Dusty rubbed the Snow Pony around her eyes, brushing the dried sweat from her face. The corners of her mouth were raw where she had fought against the bit, and her coat was stiff and shiny where Jack had hosed her down. "You dumb horse. You've learnt all your other lessons: tying up, getting washed, going on the truck, getting saddled."

The Snow Pony nestled her head into the front of Dusty's shirt, and it felt as though she was trying to hide there. Dusty thought back to the time she'd first seen her up at The Plains, wild and beautiful, happy with her pinto pal, and wished that she hadn't begged Jack to catch her. If the mare didn't turn out, what would happen to her? Would they just turn her loose again? She might never find her mate. She might not be able to survive in the wild any more.

"I'm sorry, girl," Dusty whispered in the fluffy grey ear. "It's my fault all this has happened to you, but let him ride you. It's just one more thing to learn. I know you can do it."

As Dusty climbed out of the yards she glanced back at the Snow Pony. The mare looked so sad and woebegone, standing like a waif in the dusty yards, that it brought tears to her eyes. She was still teary when she stepped into the bright fluorescent light of the kitchen and her father pulled her on to his knee.

"Don't be sad, mate. I'll give her a week. I'll ride her every day for a week, and if she hasn't come good by then we'll have to give her a miss. Okay? Do you think that's fair enough?"

28

Dusty nodded her head sadly. It was fair, but it wasn't hopeful. She didn't think the Snow Pony would ever let Jack ride her.

❧

The Snow Pony stood in the furthest corner of the yards with her rump turned towards the house. Her hay lay uneaten on the ground, even though she looked pinched and hungry. She didn't turn as Dusty walked across the yard, calling her softly, but when the girl's arms circled her neck she sighed and dropped her head. The week was up. Today, when Jack had ridden her, she had bucked as furiously as she had on the first day.

"Poor girl." Dusty rubbed her behind the ear. "You can't help it, can you?" As she stood there in the warm spring evening, Dusty knew she was going to do the thing she had wanted to do ever since her father had started breaking in the Snow Pony.

She fetched the tack box from the shed and brushed the dust and dried sweat from the mare's coat, combed her mane and tail and picked out her hooves. She took the crupper off the saddle. She knew the Snow Pony hated it. Then she saddled her, carefully smoothing all the creases out of the saddle blanket and lifting the saddle up slowly on to her back, with the girth, breastplate, and stirrups folded over the top so nothing would flap or frighten her. She measured the stirrup leathers against her arm and shortened them to her length, then buckled up the chin strap of her riding helmet and peered through the rails of the yards towards the house. Good, no one was outside. Her parents would kill her if they knew what she was doing. A voice in her head was saying they were right, it was a stupid idea, a childish fantasy that she could ride a horse that had defeated her father. But another voice, a louder voice, said she *could* do it, that the Snow Pony trusted her, would do anything for her.

Dusty gathered the reins and a big clump of mane on the Snow Pony's wither, and moved in very close to her shoulder. "Steady, girl." She put her foot in the stirrup, keeping her back facing the Snow Pony's head, and gently swung up into the saddle, trying to copy her father's calm, economical movement.

The mare didn't react as Dusty settled into the saddle and felt frantically for her off-side stirrup. Usually her boot slid straight in, but this was Jack's saddle, and the iron was in a slightly different spot. "Hang on, girl." She was shaking like a leaf. So much for staying calm so that the Snow Pony wouldn't get upset, she thought.

"Gotcha!" Her foot finally found the stirrup. She took a huge breath, then let it out again, then just sat there, breathing in and blowing out until she stopped shaking.

The Snow Pony slowly turned her head and looked quizzically at her boot as if to say, "Are you right? Are you ready now?" Dusty laughed out loud and suddenly it felt as if everything was going to be all right. She clicked her tongue and squeezed the Snow Pony with her legs, and the mare moved forward. She felt different from any other horse Dusty had ever ridden: narrow, wobbly, and unsure, as though she didn't know where to go. Horses that were used to being ridden moved off with a purpose—they knew they were going somewhere—but this mare was like a ship without a rudder. Dusty guided her more

30

deliberately with her legs and reins, and it felt as if she was exaggerating everything, but the Snow Pony seemed to like it. It didn't feel as though she was going to buck.

Dusty rode her around the yard three times, then turned and went the other way. She stopped and backed her up, then went forward again. The Snow Pony did everything she asked. Finally, Dusty plucked up courage and pushed her into a trot. They did circles and figure-eights in the yard, and all the while the Snow Pony had one ear back listening to Dusty's voice. "Good girl, good girl." They were going so beautifully that Dusty thought they might as well canter. So she sat down in the saddle, clicked her tongue and the Snow Pony broke into a canter. It felt as though she was floating, flying through the dust-filled air like an angel. She brought her back to a trot, turned, and cantered that way too, then trotted down to a halt.

Dusty felt so happy it seemed as though her heart was going to jump out of her chest. "Oh, you good thing, you good girl!" She reached down and patted the Snow Pony on her sweating neck. When she looked up she could see the lights of the house glowing yellow in the evening light. "Come on, girl," she said to her horse. "Let's go and show them."

She rode across the open space between the yards and the house in a wobbly line. Everything was very still. The dogs watched from their kennels, without moving. The Snow Pony seemed even more unsure in this much bigger space, and she hung back as they approached the house.

"Okay, girl," Dusty soothed, nudging her gently with her heels all the while. "Good girl, there's the gate, and that's the garage, and here's the house." She could see Rita in the kitchen, through the gaps in the hedge. "Whoa, girl, I'm going to yell."

Tabby walked out the gate and sat in front of the Snow Pony, staring up with her solemn cat's eyes, and the mare put her head down to look closer, snorting softly.

"Mum!" Dusty saw her mother look up. "Mum, come out here! Get Dad to come too. I want to show you something!" She heard them step off the back porch and she called softly to them as she gathered her reins. "Talk to me as you come, so she doesn't get a fright."

"What are you doing, you crazy girl? What have you . . ." Rita's voice died away as she walked through the gate, and she and Jack stood together in the twilight, staring at Dusty on the Snow Pony. Dusty studied her father's face anxiously. She had never defied him over anything important, so she didn't know how he'd react. He had an expression on his face that she'd never seen before, but he wasn't angry. He looked gobsmacked. The shock on Rita's face slowly turned into a huge smile.

"You're incredible. You're a little bugger, but you're incredible." She turned to Jack and poked him in the side. "You've got to be proud of her."

And Jack slowly smiled too, nodding his head as if to say, yep, you're right.

5

A One-Girl Horse

The Snow Pony never tried to buck Dusty off. When she was frightened, she shied or leapt like a scalded cat, but she never tried to lose her. The mare seemed to know that she was Dusty's horse, and hers alone.

That spring, when the weather was so hot and dry it almost felt like summer, Dusty rode her nearly every day and the Snow Pony learnt something new each time. Jack didn't offer help or advice, and Dusty didn't ask for any.

"It's as though he hates me riding her," she complained to Rita one afternoon. "As though we're invisible."

Rita sighed. "He's got a lot on his mind at the moment, with this dry weather. The dams are only half full and summer hasn't even started. And you know what he's like. He hates getting beaten and he's not very good at giving compliments, but I heard him talking to Barney yesterday and he couldn't stop going on about what a fantastic job you were doing. He's so proud of you."

"Hmm." Dusty shrugged her shoulders. "I guess he'll tell me one day."

After school, Stewie sometimes caught his pony and rode with Dusty. They invented a game called Horse Tiggy where one gave the other a five-minute start, then tried to find and tag them. They hid in the garden, the sheds, under the willows that lined the creek—anywhere that provided cover. Stewie's pinto pony, Tarzan, was so small he could hide in tiny places. Once he hid in the woodshed, and another time, when Rita was out, Stewie rode him right into the house and hid in their bedroom. Dusty saw the curtains move and thought it was the cat, until finally it got too much for Tarzan and he whinnied to the Snow Pony, and gave them away. The Snow Pony couldn't fit into such small places but she would go anywhere Dusty asked her to, so they found wonderfully unexpected places to hide, like in the back of the truck or on top of the woodpile. She still leapt like a grasshopper if she was frightened, but Dusty had learnt how to hang on.

One night at the dinner table, when they were talking about that evening's Tiggy session, Rita butted in. "This game is a great way for you to get to know the Snow Pony, but you realise she's too good to be just a fun horse, don't you? I think it's time you started schooling her on the flat and over jumps." She turned to Jack. "What do you think?"

He nodded his head, still chewing. "If she can jump anywhere near as well as you think she can, she should win every competition between here and Melbourne." He forced a smile. "It'd be good to have some extra cash coming in."

Dusty stared at her plate, shocked to think that her father was counting on her to earn money. It was something they never talked about. In the past there had always seemed to be enough of it. If she and Stewie

34

needed something they always got it: new shoes, new riding boots, new bathers. The money was never mentioned. Lately, though, her parents were forever discussing how much things cost. She suddenly recalled the hard time she and Sally gave Megan Timms about her holey runners in grade four, and blushed because now it was like that for them, the Rileys. There just wasn't enough money to pay for everything.

After dinner, when they'd cleared the table and done the dishes, Dusty sat at one end of the kitchen table and did her geography assignment, and Jack and Rita sat at the other end with piles of bills, writing figures in columns and arguing. Rita wanted to set up a new business, Riley's Mountain Rides, and take people from the city riding on the high plains, but Jack wouldn't hear of it.

"I'm not running a dude ranch. This land has provided a living for our family for generations without us having to play cowboys."

Rita pushed back her chair and pursed her lips. "Well I don't know what you think we're going to live on, Mr. High-and-Mighty. The whole state is short of rain, so we're not going to get a lot for our calves this year. And look at this." Rita slammed her account book on the table. "I've only had half the normal amount of horses to school this year. No one around here has spare cash for non-essentials. You've got to access all that money in Melbourne. People there have more money than they know what to do with." She gave Dusty a sneaky smile. "They'd pay heaps to go riding with a mountain legend."

Jack stood up and walked outside, slamming the door

35

behind him. Dusty kept on with her homework, but it felt as though Jack's temper hung above her like a vapour trail.

"Why is he like that, Mum?"

Rita looked up from the accounts. "What do you mean? Like what?"

Dusty pulled a face. "You know, prickly, uptight, proud. Everything always has to be done *his* way."

"Oh, sweetie," Rita stretched her head back and shook her halo of curls, as though she was trying to jiggle her thoughts into line. "He *is* all those things, but he's also strong and honest and true and intelligent. And he can be pretty funny, too."

Dusty narrowed her eyes and tried to remember the last time Jack had made her laugh. "Don't fob me off, Mum. You know what I mean. It's like he's separate from everyone else. He's not part of the community. He won't join the CFA because he reckons they're all idiots, and he's not in Rotary or any of those things. We've got heaps of second cousins but we hardly know them . . ."

"All right, all right. I do know what you mean." Rita pushed her chair back. "I guess part of it is that his dad was like that. Proud, aloof, had to be the best. A lovely man if you were on his side, but no time for anyone he didn't respect. He played the violin like an angel. And his mother died when he was just a little boy, so there was no one to soften that pride. And then there's the way she died."

"It was a car accident, wasn't it?"

"Yes, and somehow it was Jack's uncle's fault. That put a rift in the family that's never healed." Rita reached over the bills and ruffled Dusty's glossy black hair. "They say you look just like her, and she was a gun rider too . . . but your father, no, he is the way he is and that's that. He's got good friends all over the place, from boarding school, and ag. college, cattlemen, bushies. He's not a snob, he's just choosy. But . . ." Rita looked straight into Dusty's eyes with her own level green ones, "he loves us dearly. He'd do anything for you kids. Don't forget that."

∾

Dusty began to school the Snow Pony that summer. Under Rita's instruction, she walked and trotted and cantered in circles, bending and flexing until she was soft and round. She was so light on her feet that Dusty felt as though she were sitting on the shoulders of a ballet dancer.

"She feels beautiful, Mum, you should have a ride," she said as she rode up to Rita at the end of a session, and Rita accepted the offer because the mare looked like a dream. But when she rode her it was more like a nightmare. The Snow Pony rushed around the arena as though the devil was on her back, and Rita was glad to get off.

She shook her head as she handed the reins to Dusty. "I always thought it was nonsense that some horses could only be ridden by one person. I thought a good rider could get any horse to behave. But this mare's weird. She really does go only for you."

Dusty's heart swelled a little bit, but Rita frowned. "I don't like it. Not for the same reason as Dad; not because I can't stand being beaten. I don't care about that. No, it's more that her refusal to go nicely for anyone but you indicates how wilful she is, and that frightens me. There's a wildness in her that makes her unsafe. I'm afraid that one day you'll get hurt." She laughed at Dusty's gloomy face. "It's all right, mate. I'm not going to stop you riding her or anything like that. I just worry about you, that's all. Come on, let's school her over some trot poles."

∾

The Snow Pony turned out to be a jumping machine. She never refused a jump or ran out, and she hated touching the poles with her hooves. Dusty's biggest problem was slowing her down enough to take the tight bends in a showjumping course. They started competing towards the end of summer, and sometimes the Snow Pony's speed was so terrifying that Rita had to cover her eyes. Dusty won every junior jumping event she entered, and blitzed the field in her first maiden D grade, for horses that hadn't won at that level before. As they quickly accumulated D grade points, winning at every show, people started to come up to Dusty, asking her about her horse. Everybody loved the story of the Snow Pony.

"Winning's fun, isn't it?" Dusty propped her feet on the dashboard of the old truck as Rita drove home after their final D grade competition. The Snow Pony had notched up too many points to stay in that class, and the luscious blue ribbons she had won hung from the rear vision mirror. The prize money was in an envelope in the glove box and Dusty felt on top of the world.

"Yep," Rita replied. "Winning's great, but you have to learn how to lose, too."

"Mum! That's not fair. I've been riding those learners of yours for years. I know how to lose."

Rita laughed. "I suppose you do. But it will feel

different, losing on the Snow Pony. It means so much more to you. And now you're in C grade it won't be so easy. The jumps will be bigger and the course will be tighter. You won't be able to motorbike the way you have been. You'll have to slow down, get more control."

∾

Sally rang up to ask her over for the weekend. "I never see you any more, Dusty." She pretended to sob. "The Snow Pony's stolen you away from me. Ha ha ha. But seriously, I'm going away to boarding school in two weeks and we'll never see each other then. Can't you come over? Can't you miss showjumping? Just one weekend?"

Dusty twisted the phone cord with her free hand. She *had* been neglecting Sally lately, and she felt guilty that she'd hardly missed her at all because she'd been so involved with the Snow Pony. "I can't, Sal. It's the Bankstown Show next weekend, my first C grade."

Sally was silent at the other end of the phone.

"But, hey, why don't you come? You could watch us jump, and then we could muck around at the sideshows, like we used to when we were little. Go on the flying horses, play the clowns. Remember that time we crawled under the back of the boxing tent and saw that guy get knocked out?"

"Yeah, and we got the giggles because you said he'd wet his pants, and then they threw us out." Sally laughed at the memory. "Okay, I'll come on the bus tomorrow night. It should be fun. See ya." Sally hung up and hoped it would be fun, not Dusty glaring at her every time she moved the wrong way near that stupid horse.

6
The Accident

Sally and Stew sat together outside the arena, watching Dusty and the Snow Pony jump. On the other side of the showgrounds the sideshows and rides blared out noise and action, but here, under the giant cypress trees, it was quiet and shady. Everybody here was watching the showjumping. Dusty had already been in one event, the C grade Table A, and had her first taste of failure on the Snow Pony. It was just as Rita said: you simply couldn't get around a C grade course as fast as the Snow Pony had been going. The course was too tight and the jumps too big. Dusty's approach to the jumps became more and more angled until finally the Snow Pony missed a jump altogether. When Sally and Stew got back to the truck, Dusty had calmed down, though her eyes were red, and Sally guessed she had been crying, tears of frustration. Dusty always cried when she got mad.

"You have to sing," Rita was saying. "Sing to give yourself a rhythm, and she'll pick it up. Come on, try. 'If you go out in the woods today, bom bom, you'd better not go alone. Bom bom . . .' See, it works, try that when you go out next time."

Now they were watching her second event, and the singing seemed to be working. The Snow Pony moved around the jumping course at a steady pace. She was still very fast, but she wasn't racing and plunging, just gliding along, flying over the jumps as though they were hardly there.

"She's wicked, isn't she?" Stewie whispered.

Sally nodded. She could see why Dusty was so obsessed with her beautiful horse. They looked *great*.

"It looks like they're dancing, with all those curves."

"Yeah, Mum says that showjumping's just half circles with jumps in them. She says if you can get the circles right, you're nearly there." Stewie pulled his cap lower over his eyes. "It doesn't seem to work for me, though. I always get lost. Dad reckons I need a horse that can read the numbers on the jumps."

They stopped talking as Dusty finished her round, and after a little while Sally became aware of something poking her in the ribs. It was Stewie, staring at her, wriggling his eyebrows and turning his head to one side like a lunatic. Sally leant forward and realised that the elderly couple sitting there were talking about Dusty.

"No, young Jack . . . from out at Banjo . . . yes . . . his daughter. And her mother was Rita Poole before she was married. She took showjumpers all over the place when she was younger. She doesn't compete any more, but I hear she gets young horses going. She'd have done all the work on that mare . . ." The loudspeaker drowned the conversation for a few seconds. " . . . at least twenty grand. You'd sell her to Europe for easily that much."

When Dusty got back to the truck with her blue sash

41

they were waiting impatiently for her.

"Dusty! Dusty!" Stewie was jumping up and down like a flea. "We heard some people saying that you could sell the Snow Pony for twenty thousand dollars!"

Dusty jumped off and started to take off the saddle. "What's he talking about, Sally?"

"This old couple next to us were talking . . ."

"Yeah," Stewie butted in. "We were earsdropping!"

Dusty gave him a little shove as she passed with her saddle. "It's eavesdropping, idiot. And I could never sell the Snow Pony, not for any money. She only goes for me. Isn't that right, Mum?"

Rita nodded and just then Jack appeared. He had told Dusty he'd try to call in and watch her.

"That was a beautiful round, Dusty." He patted the Snow Pony's neck. "You and Mum have got her going like a dream."

"Thanks, Dad." Dusty hugged him.

This was the first time he'd come to watch her jump. With the drought stretching on for another summer, he was always too busy to come to the shows with Rita and Dusty. Or that's what he said. Dusty thought he was embarrassed to come, as if he felt he were hanging around like a bad smell, sweating on her winning. There was no doubt the money the Snow Pony had won made life easier, but Jack seemed to be ashamed of it at the same time. Rita kept an account book with all the sums recorded, so Dusty would get her money back, with interest, when the drought was over, but for now it all went to the farm.

"Dad!" Stewie starting shaking Jack's arm. "Guess

what Sal and I heard some people . . ."

Dusty stepped between her father and Stewie and glared at him. "Shut up!" she mouthed. She didn't want Jack to know how valuable people thought her horse was. She wasn't sure she could trust him if it came to a choice between the Snow Pony and money.

The sideshows and stalls were fun, even with just a few dollars to spend, and Sally always made things interesting. They wandered through the dog section, peeling off sticky wisps of pink fairy floss and eating it as they went.

"I'm telling you, Dusty, all the dog owners look like their dogs. Look at that one!" She squealed with laughter and Dusty turned to see a stumpy man, with five double chins, sitting with his bulldog. They giggled together as they matched the dogs with their owners: a tiny woman with fluffy hair grooming her poodle, a lanky girl with sad eyes and her red setter. As they passed the old grandstand several people stopped Dusty to congratulate her.

"I hope you're going in the Grand Parade," old Mr. Wilson said to her. He was from Banjo and had been on the Bankstown Show committee for years.

"Yeah, Dusty, you have to," Sal was excited. "I'll take a photo as you go past and I can have it on my wall at school."

It really hit Dusty then that Sally was going away, and how much she was going to miss her. If Sally were coming to Bankstown Secondary College with her this year it would be a breeze, but without her—Dusty couldn't imagine school without Sally. There'd be no one to talk to on the hour-long bus trip, she wouldn't know anyone, and the worst thing was, Sally wouldn't be there to make her laugh. Sally changed her somehow, made her a smarter, funnier person. By herself, Dusty sometimes felt like a clod, a hillbilly.

The Grand Parade moved slowly around the arena, all the prize winners showing off their ribbons. The cattle came first, led by their owners in white coats; then the led horses, the ridden horses, and the harness horses. Dusty rode on the outside, nearest the rail, so Sally could get a good shot of her. The Snow Pony felt like a coiled spring under her as the crowds cheered and clapped and the loudspeakers blared out a description of the passing parade. Dusty was peering across at the other side of the oval, where an enormous Friesian bull was bellowing like a foghorn, so she didn't see Sally duck under the fence and race towards her for a better shot. When the flash went off, the Snow Pony spun and ran so fast that at first nobody knew what had happened. She bolted through the steward's area in the middle of the arena, and Dusty felt a sting on her cheek as they flew past the loudspeaker van. The Snow Pony came back to her then and Dusty pulled her up and turned to rejoin their place in the parade.

"Whoa, girl, it's all right. Just Sal and her camera."

She didn't realise anything was wrong until a steward walked towards her, staring in shock. Then she felt something wet on her shoulder, and when she looked down her riding jacket was covered with blood. She put her hand to her cheek. It felt like a flap. And when she pulled her hand away, it was bloody, too.

∾

Dusty peered into the tiny hand mirror and tried to catch the reflection of the side of her face in the bathroom

44

mirror. The scar was red and angry-looking, even though the stitches had come out last week. It angled in from below her cheekbone, running towards the corner of her mouth in a straight line for about five centimetres. It looked ugly. Dusty put the hand mirror down and turned to face herself in the big mirror. Straight on it didn't look bad at all, almost hidden in the hollow of her cheek. It was two weeks since the accident, since the wire poking out from the loudspeaker van had sliced her face open as the Snow Pony bolted past. What had happened afterwards was a blur: people crowded around her, the ambulance, the helicopter to Melbourne, doctors, the operation, nurses, and hospital. Sally and Milo had come to see her with flowers and a cow painting, and Sally had wept and wept, seeing her friend's bandaged face. Dusty tried to cheer her up, but Sally was inconsolable that she had caused the accident.

"Sal, it's not your fault. It's just the way the Snow Pony is. She could have bolted like that at anything. It's like what you told us about friends, Milo, you have to take the whole package. I love her for her brilliance, so I've just got to put up with her craziness." She looked out the window at the city shimmering in the summer heat. "Mum and Dad want me to give her up. They think she's too dangerous. Mum's promised not to let Dad do anything until I get home, but there's no way he's going to sell her, or turn her loose. She's my horse and I'm going to keep riding her. We're going to be champions, the Snow Pony and me."

In the end, when she'd come home from hospital, there'd been no flaming row. Two hours into the drive back from Melbourne the silence in the car became heavy with the topic of the Snow Pony and Dusty got in first. "I'm not going to give her up. I'm going to keep riding her and keep jumping her."

Another twenty minutes of silence followed that statement until Rita cleared her throat.

"Okay. I'm not sure what you think about this, Jack." She looked at the side of his face, his eyes concentrating on the road. "You can keep riding her, and keep jumping her. I know how much she means to you. But realise the danger. If she'd been any closer to that van you would have been killed." She looked at Dusty over the back of her seat and her eyes were full of tears. "We could have lost you, Dusty. That mustn't happen again. No, ride her, jump her, but stay away from pressure situations as much as you can. And she only has one more chance. Another crazy stunt like that and she goes."

∾

The day Dusty got her stitches out she came home from the doctor's and went straight outside to ride. The Snow Pony flew over the baked summer ground like a bird as they galloped up the rise behind the house, and Dusty found herself grinning with joy. The scar pulled against her smile but it didn't matter. She had a scar but she also had a wonderful horse.

7
New School

When Dusty started at Bankstown Secondary, it was about as bad as she expected. She arrived a week late, because of the accident, and everyone seemed to have a friend except her. It was a huge change, going from the tiny one-teacher school at Banjo, where she'd known everyone since kindergarten, to the big central college with five hundred students.

Sally had gone to boarding school at the end of January, and Dusty had already got two letters from her. She wrote about how much she missed home, but the letters were also full of her new life and the girls she shared a dormitory with. Dusty had always assumed that she and Sally would go away to boarding school together. They used to spend hours inventing glamorous adventures they could have in their new life in the city. But the drought, which had lasted for two years now, meant there was no money for private schooling. And secretly, Dusty was relieved. She couldn't imagine being away from the Snow Pony for a whole term.

She was miserable at Bankstown Secondary. Without Sally to plot and giggle with, without Sally to send up the teachers and put the cool kids in their place, Dusty felt as lonely as Rita's post in the paddock. The kids in her form talked about TV shows and bands she'd never heard of. They read hip magazines, wore trendy clothes, and knew all the latest songs. She couldn't even watch *Rage* on TV, because every Saturday morning they were up at dawn and off to another show. Even though she loved competing on the Snow Pony, she wished there was room in her life for something else.

One of the boys in her class, Danny Connelly, started calling her Slim, as in Slim Dusty, and soon all his mates were doing it, too. When Dusty passed them in the corridor they'd all start to sing "The Pub with No Beer," then howl with laughter as she walked away. When she looked at her reflection straight on, her scar didn't seem too bad, but she knew that from the side it was drastic, slicing through her dark features like a lightning bolt. Everybody talked about it. Some girls came straight out and asked what had happened, others whispered together, then stopped when she walked into the room. One girl, Shannon, even called her Scarface. Dusty started to wear her hair loose, so she could let it fall over that side of her face. She decided that the only way to survive school was to treat it as a chore. Rita drove her into Banjo to catch the bus in the morning, and after she kissed her mother goodbye it was "survival mode" until she got off the bus in the afternoon. She read for the hour it took to get to Bankstown, then went to the school library, read again, went to her locker, went to class, then read all the way home again. Sometimes the "good" girls from her class asked her to have lunch with them, but most days she sat by herself and read. She was powering through books.

Dusty wasn't the only loner at the school. From behind her hair, she watched kids hanging around the edges of groups, trying to be part of a gang, but Dusty would rather have died than done that. There was another girl, Jade, who always seemed to be on her own, but she was a year ahead of Dusty, and she was hardly ever at school anyway. "Her mother's a hippy, she's so trippy," Dusty heard Danny Connelly snigger once as Jade walked past.

Dusty and Sally wrote to each other every week, and it seemed that as Dusty's life got worse, Sally's got better. Dusty tried not to feel jealous when she read about shopping and sport and midnight feasts, but it felt as if Sally were moving into a different world. Dusty lived for the weekends, when she, Rita, and Stewie would head off to a show.

The Snow Pony was jumping better all the time, although she didn't win every event. Dusty learnt to lose, learnt to accept that sometimes things just didn't go right. She still rode Rita's learners in the novice events, so by the end of the day she was exhausted. Stewie had started to ride Tarzan in the novelty events—the bending race, the flag and barrel—and the first time he won a ribbon his smile went from ear to ear. Jack never came with them to the shows; he was busy cutting lucerne and getting things ready for when the cows came home. There was no feed for them at The Willows because the paddocks were bare, so he was trying to buy hay as well, but the drought was so widespread that the price was astronomical. He was getting grumpier and grumpier. He was always snapping at Stewie, and it seemed to Dusty that he hardly spoke to her.

"I reckon he feels like a failure," she whispered to Stewie one night as they lay in bed listening to him arguing with Rita about what to do. "He's always been the man, the boss, and now he's relying on me, his kid, for money."

School was so awful that Dusty tried to stay home as often as she could, and when it was time to bring the cows and calves down from The Plains it was a joy to take a week off. They sat around the kitchen table and planned the trip. The four of them were going. Dusty remembered the funny times they'd had together on the road in the past and hoped this trip would be as good.

"I wonder if the pinto, Hillbilly, will still be there," she said to Rita. "I wonder if the Snow Pony will remember him."

Rita looked at Jack and then at Dusty. "You're not taking the Snow Pony."

Dusty started to argue, but Rita cut her off.

"This isn't open to discussion, Dusty. Your father and I have decided. It's only a year since she came down, and we think it would be asking for trouble to take her back up. You wouldn't want to lose her."

Dusty looked at her parents and she could see that they were serious. And it would be terrible if her beautiful mare ran off with the brumbies. Life would be unbearable without the Snow Pony.

"Okay," she conceded. "I'll take Spook, then." But one day, she thought to herself, one day I'll ride the Snow Pony on the high plains.

The show season stopped soon after they brought the cows and calves down from The Plains, and then Dusty was flat out helping with the cattle. The calves were weaned, and the day they were separated from their mothers the bellowing and bawling from the yards was deafening. She and Jack worked in the yards together, drafting the cows and calves, deciding which ones to cull, picking out some promising heifers to add to the herd. As Rita predicted, the calf sales brought them little reward. Nobody had any feed, so the demand for store cattle was low, and their cheque was only two-thirds what it had been the year before. It was a pathetic income for a year's work.

After the sales, winter crept in, as though the gloom had affected the weather. Now, going to school was even worse for Dusty; getting on the bus in the dark, coming home in the dark. The Snow Pony stood in her paddock for days at a time without being ridden. It was cold and it was dark, but it still didn't rain. Sally still wrote every week and even though Dusty felt envious, it was great to be able to be part of her life through the mail. Sally had come home for Easter and brought a friend with her: Meena, whose parents lived in Hong Kong. Dusty went and stayed for a couple of nights and it was good fun, but it was different. She guessed it would always be different for her and Sally from now on.

Spring came, and as soon as the snow had melted from The Plains they drove the cows and calves up there, anxious to get them away from the dirt patch that The

grandstand, half-dancing as they picked up the rhythms of the music. They were as colourful and noisy as a flock of parrots, and laden down with stuff from the sideshows: crazy hats, over-size glasses, fairy floss, plastic windmills, and show bags.

"Hey, Dusty!" They stopped and looked up at her as though she were a sideshow herself. "Wotcha doing up there? Why're ya wearing a tie, ya dag?" Shannon nudged the others, and laughed.

Dusty shrugged. "I've been riding, showjumping. You have to wear a tie."

"Far out." Danny Connelly peered up at her over his sunglasses. "That's as bad as a school uniform. I have enough of that during the week, man!" He exploded into laughter, and Dusty felt like punching him on the nose.

"So, did you win?" He was still there, hands on his hips, grinning at her.

"Yeah, I did actually." I won two hundred and fifty dollars, you smarty, thought Dusty, but I'm not going to tell *you* that. Let them think she was a dork. They had no idea about showjumping—how difficult, fast, and exciting it was.

"Cool. Oh well, catch ya." As they walked on, Shannon said something Dusty couldn't hear, and the group howled with laughter.

It was times like this that she missed Sally the most. She didn't even want these stupid kids as friends, she just wanted *them* to want *her*. But she was getting used to being on her own.

They stopped in front of the purple tent and Dusty could hear the girls going on in that gooey way that made her want to vomit. "Ooooh! How beautiful is this? Ooooh! I looove that colour! Ooooh! That really suits you!" Jeannie was playing up to them, whirling, swirling, showing them dresses, candles, crystals, and shawls, but Jade was standing to one side, tidying the jewellery cabinet, and the kids ignored her.

Dusty was going home with money in her pocket — two hundred and fifty dollars that would go straight into the farm bank account. She would have loved to go into the purple tent and spend some of it on jewellery and groovy Indian clothes, but she was too shy. She always felt like such a hick in her riding clothes. And besides, her family depended on that money. She stayed in the grandstand for a while, watching the crowds drift past, listening to Jade's mother rave on, then wandered back to the truck and her solitary showjumping life.

8

Tough Times in Banjo

That summer, when Dusty turned fourteen, was the driest for years. The creek slowed to a trickle, the dams were nearly empty, and the hills around the house crouched like thirsty animals, holding the folds of the valley in their giant paws. Battered old red gums dotted the slopes, and ugly patches of red earth showed through the tawny cover where cattle had chewed the dry grass to nothing. The only green on the farm was the ribbon of willows that lined the road and the paddock of lucerne growing on the irrigated land beside the creek. Fortunately for the Rileys, their cattle were up on the high plains. All that remained on the farm were Dusty's house cow, Spot, the horses, and a mob of scrawny sheep that had provided their meat for two years now. Killers, these sheep were called, and Dusty hated them. Sometimes, when her mum put tea on the table and it was chops again, Dusty wanted to throw them out the window and scream.

There used to be a school bus that ran from Banjo out to their farm, but so many families had moved away from the valley that the education department closed the service down. You had to have at least twelve kids to get a

9

The Gelantipy Cows

Dusty stepped off the Bankstown bus and walked past Christanis' milk bar, studying the footpath as though it held the secrets of the universe, determined not to let her eyes veer right to the trays of lollies in the window. She was starving. Before things got so bad, when she was still at Banjo Primary, she and Stew and the other kids used to race each other from school to the milk bar steps. An icy pole, a packet of chicken chips, a licorice strap—there were always a few coins in your pocket, or Mrs. Christani would put it on their account.

"Don't worry," Jack used to joke. "Ze Count will pay for it."

But Ze Count couldn't pay any more. It hadn't rained in Banjo for nearly three years now and it was as though the drought had sucked all the money, as well as the moisture, out of the land. The Rileys owed the Christanis so much that they were too embarrassed to go into the shop. Old Mrs. Christani had shuffled out one day, wiping her hands on her apron as Rita waited to pick Dusty up from the bus, and taken her by the hand. "I know you cannot pay now, but I know you will when you can. You are not the only ones. But please, still come in, to buy for cash. We have no business because everyone is so full of shame."

Rita did go in after that, to buy the papers and bread, but the kids never had money for lollies now, so it was better not to look.

Dusty sat on the seat outside the milk bar, sliding a stone from side to side with her feet. The first week back at Bankstown Secondary hadn't been as bad as last year, but it still wasn't any fun. She knew some kids now, to talk to and have lunch with, but there was nobody she felt really close to. That last fun week of the holidays with Sally made the dullness of school seem even worse. Jade, the girl with the hippy mother, had only been at school one day, but Dusty was too embarrassed to go and sit with her anyway.

Dusty could see their car driving up from the school, her mum behind the wheel and Stewie in the passenger seat. He loved getting in first and pinching that front seat. As she watched them approach she realised something was wrong. Stewie was as stiff as a little soldier and Rita was slumped in her seat, holding the wheel so carelessly it looked as though she could hardly bother to steer.

"What's wrong?" Dusty asked the question before she was properly in the car. Neither of them answered, and her heart started to pound. "Is Dad all right?"

"Yes, yes. He's fine." Rita reassured her but she didn't turn, just kept staring out the windscreen like a zombie. It was Stewie who twisted in his seat belt until he was facing her, his eyes wide with the terrible knowledge. "All the Gelantipy cows are dead."

"What?"

The Gelantipy cows had limped down their road last week, like walking bags of bones. It was tragic to see beautiful cows in such a pitiful condition. A farmer from the little mountain town of Gelantipy had "gone on the road" with his twenty-five cows, in a desperate effort to find feed for them. It was a common enough thing in tough times, to walk your cattle slowly along the roads and byways so they could eat the grass on the roadside. Some people trucked their cattle hundreds of kilometres to areas where the rains had been good, and entrusted them to contract drovers. This man had no money for that, so he had just headed south with his cows, but he was too late. Every scrap of dry grass had been eaten months ago.

Dusty was with Jack when he drove down to the crossing, where the man had set up camp for the night.

"Gidday." The men nodded to each other.

Dusty stared at the man. He was as skinny as his cows.

"I'll open that gate for you if you like. There's no feed in there, but the creek's a bit wider for them to get a drink." Jack invited him to share dinner with the family and by the end of the night had offered to buy the cows. "I can't pay you now," he offered the man, "but if you can wait until this is over, I'll pay you a fair price for them then. You won't even cover your cartage if you send them to market."

They negotiated an agreement right there on the kitchen table, and both parties were happy with the deal. Jack was pleased to have the beautiful cows to add to his herd—even though they were skin-and-bone—and the poor farmer was glad that his cows would be fed.

"We've been baling lucerne all summer," Rita said. "We're on to our third cut, and we've bought a shed full of hay. That should see them through the winter."

Now they were dead. How could twenty-five cows be dead?

"What happened?"

Stewie looked across at Rita but she didn't speak, so he answered. "They got into the lucerne paddock. Dad left the gate open and they gutsed themselves and died of bloat. He found them this morning. They look awful, all blown up like monsters."

Digger slunk out to meet Dusty, when they got home, with his tail tucked between his legs.

"Hi, boy." She reached down to pat him. He looked as sad as she felt. All those beautiful old cows! From beyond the flat paddock she could hear the groaning and clanking of a bulldozer at work.

"He's digging a pit." Rita slammed the car door. "We can't burn them because of the fire restrictions, so he's borrowed Vince's dozer."

∾

Jack didn't come back to the house that night until Rita bumped over the paddocks in the ute and insisted that he stop working. Stewie was in bed, but Dusty had lingered over her homework so she had an excuse to be up. She heard him kicking his boots off on the back porch and got up to hug him as he came into the kitchen. He looked like a survivor from a desert war, and his singlet smelt of sweat and dust and diesel.

"I'm sorry, Dad."

He patted her lightly on the back and stepped out of her

arms, then stood like a zombie, bloodshot eyes blinking in the harsh fluorescent light. He started to speak but choked on the words. A trail of tears cut through the dust on his face. It frightened Dusty more than any of his rages ever had.

When she got up in the morning he was gone, and the sound of the bulldozer working drifted intermittently into the house. School, and the bus before and after, went by in a blur; all she could think about was those bloated cows and her family unravelling. When they got home she fed the horses and her cow and went straight inside to do homework. She didn't want to be on the farm, so she lost herself in *To Kill a Mockingbird,* which her class was reading for English. It was good to share someone else's troubles.

∾

Jack didn't speak during dinner except to ask for salt. He was scrubbed clean. The dirt under his nails and in-grained in his hands were the only remainder of the filth that had covered him last night. The dozer was back at Vince's and the lucerne was springing back from where it had been crushed. It was as though the Gelantipy cows had never existed.

A car turned off the road, the bridge rattled, and head-lights swung past the kitchen window. Rita walked out to turn the back light on. Dusty looked at her father. He was rubbing his face in his hands, looking as if he didn't want to see anyone.

"Barney!" Rita's voice carried back to the kitchen. "How are you, mate?"

Barney's reply sounded more like a growl than words.

He looked like a bear and he sounded like a bear. Jack rose to shake hands as the big man entered the kitchen, and met his eyes for a brief second.

"Bad luck about the cows." He tossed a parcel on to the table. "I bought some flathead tails for you."

It was typical that Barney would be the one person who called in to cheer up her dad, thought Dusty. He had been their friend ever since he bought the block next door to them ten years ago. Originally from the city, he loved the valley, and the Rileys were the closest thing he had to a family. Jack had been scornful of his ignorance when he first arrived, but Barney's sheer goodwill made it impossible not to like him. Over the years he had experimented with all sorts of bizarre farming enterprises—growing aloe vera, raising emus, and lately alpacas—but he also ran a small herd of cows which Jack managed for him. He had always insisted on paying Jack, and the money had been a godsend. Barney had plenty of money. He worked offshore on the oil rig; two weeks on and two weeks off. He always called in when he came ashore, always with a slab of beer, a crayfish, a pile of magazines. Lately, Jack had been as morose and bitter with him as he was with everyone, but Barney wasn't put off.

"Put the kettle on, Stew," said Rita. "And tell us what you've been up to, Barney. We need distracting." Rita loved Barney's stories.

"Well, I have got a story, but it's a terrible thing. Perhaps you should go to bed, Stewie."

Stewie let out an I-hope-you're-joking laugh, and Rita backed him up. "He'll be okay, Barney. He's a big boy now."

66

"All right then." Barney cleared his throat. "Well, I was in my hole, my room, last Thursday out on the rig, and I heard this shocking noise. I raced out and Serg, one of the riggers, was hanging in the stairwell. He'd hung himself with an extension cord. He was twisting and thrashing like a shark and his face was as purple as those plums."

Dusty looked at the bowl of plums in the middle of the table. A face that colour would look like something from hell.

"I grabbed my knife. Always carry my knife."

Dusty thought about how, in the old days, Jack used to laugh about Barney and his knife; ready for anything, like a boy scout. This time he was.

"I cut him down, but his colour didn't change, he still couldn't breathe. The rubber on the cable had jammed the knot. Wouldn't release. And his neck had swelled up around it. I had to cut right into the back of his neck to cut the cable."

"Gee!" Stew's eyes were huge. "Was there blood everywhere?"

"You bet. We were slipping over in it. He'll live, the doc says, just have a big scar on his neck, courtesy of me. But I don't think he'll thank me. The poor beggar had just heard his wife and kid had been killed in Sarajevo."

∾

Barney had driven off an hour ago and Dusty was nearly asleep when the rise and fall of angry voices snapped her back to full alert. She hated that sound, the sound of her parents fighting, but she couldn't help straining her ears to hear what they were saying. The conversation

67

came muffled through the bedroom wall, her mother's voice low and terse and only responding to her father's more urgent talk. He and Barney had been drinking port, and this was always how he ended up: waving goodbye to his mate as though he didn't have a worry in the world, then turning on Rita. Dusty held her breath to hear better. He was accusing Mum of flirting with Barney. Rita was staying calm, not biting back, but finally, as Dusty knew he eventually would, Jack went too far and the conversation rose to a screaming boil-over, and then she wished she couldn't hear.

Stew hopped into bed with her, sobbing, and she held him and sang right into his ear to drown out the yelling. Among the accusations, one set of words echoed through the house like a curse: "That's what you want, isn't it, Rita?" His voice was so strained and crazy it sounded as if it were being ripped out of him. "You'd be happy if I blew my brains out."

The shouting and door-slamming finally petered out to a tense silence. Stewie had gone back to sleep when Dusty heard Rita shifting junk off the bed in the spare room, and the creak of the old bed as she settled into it. Tabby meowed at the window, and Dusty got up to let her in. The creek gleamed silver in the moonlight and the outside world looked peaceful and uncomplicated.

"I don't know why you'd want to come inside," she said to the old cat as she lifted her off the windowsill. "Everyone's crazy in here."

She left Stewie in her bed and climbed into his. Her brother's cardboard space creatures hanging off the curved cast iron bedhead spun slowly above her. She couldn't sleep. Every time she shut her eyes her father's words rang out: "You'd be happy if I blew my brains out." He could kill himself any time, Dusty thought—hanging, gassing, crashing, shooting. She could never protect him, he had too many opportunities. The terror of it made her suddenly sweat, as though she had a fever. She'd heard of suicides in Banjo, in whispered conversations that stopped suddenly when she entered a room, and harsh words in the schoolyard—topped himself, necked himself—as well as unexplained farm accidents and single car fatalities. She'd always thought that the person's family had let them down, that they should have been able to save them. But now she realised how impossible the task was, to save someone who didn't want to be saved. She lay like a corpse, holding the warm cat to her chest, until sleep finally flooded her racing mind.

∾

Another day went by and Dusty couldn't have told you a single thing anyone said to her on the bus or at school. Her mind was completely occupied with thoughts of her father. He had always been so successful, so right, and so hard on no-hopers, people who made stupid mistakes—like leaving the wrong gate open, as he had done. As Rita drove them home from Banjo, Stewie in the front seat beside her, Dusty stared at the back of her mother's head, wanting to voice her fears, but it felt like a betrayal—as though she was wishing him dead. Instead, she asked casually how Jack was.

Rita was blunt. "He needs to have a good hard look at himself, if you ask me. He's always put himself above other people, even us, without meaning to. He was born

69

with a lot of talent, and born into a comfortable life. Now he's finding out what it's like for the rest of the world."

Jack's ute was gone when they got home, so Dusty caught the Snow Pony and rode out to where he had been working, in case he was still there. From a distance the grave looked like a dam bank, and a fleeting tag of hope that it was all a mistake flashed through her mind, until she looked again and knew it wasn't. She had expected the grave to be flat, for some reason, but there was a huge area of raised earth. Of course. It made sense that if you dug a hole and put twenty-five cows in it, especially bloated ones, the dirt wouldn't all fit back in the hole.

The Snow Pony snorted and shied away from the fresh earth. As she turned, Dusty dropped the reins on her neck and let her go. They cantered up the rise that looked over the house and yards, and Dusty stretched out her arms like wings, and it felt as if she were flying. The horse was so light under her, so fluid, that it didn't feel as if her hooves were touching the ground at all. The heavy evening air swirled around her, so thick you could almost see directional arrows on it, like when they learnt about vectors in science at school.

Jack's ute was still missing when Dusty cantered into the house paddock, so she fed hay to the horses and her cow. Spot would calve any day now; her udder was swollen and her bum had that wobbly look that cows get when their time is near.

Rita was setting the table when Dusty came in. There was only three of everything. "It's all right, love." Rita answered Dusty's raised eyebrow. "He's okay. He's at the pub. I think he had to face everybody straight away. He

70

couldn't bear to feel like he was hiding away while people talked about him. I rang there a while ago and Norm said he's pretty far gone and that he'll put him to bed in the back room."

After dinner, the three of them flopped together on the couch in front of the television. They didn't really watch it, just let the light and sound wash over them. Stewie got up and made one of his special hot chocolates for everyone, and they were like three little mice snuggled together safely in their peaceful house.

10
Poor Spot

At first Dusty thought the calf was all right; that the birth was progressing as it should. The cow was lying on the side of the hill, and from the fence Dusty saw her legs rise up in a straining spasm and then flop down again. As she walked closer she could see the forelegs and head protruding from the back of the cow, presented in the correct position.

Dusty had peeled an orange when she left the house, and was sucking the second half of it as she approached the cow. She felt excited about watching the calf being born. Then she caught a glimpse of red in the calf's mouth and her hopes died. A calf shouldn't have a bloody mouth. Something was wrong. Suddenly it felt awful to be eating an orange—like scoffing chips at an execution. She flung the orange segments away and hurried to the back of the cow.

The calf was dead. It was enormous, and the end of its tongue had been eaten away by foxes.

"Oh, Spot!" Dusty sobbed and rushed to the cow's head.

The heifer didn't rise. Her eye was dull with pain. Dusty

remembered her own bed last night, warm and toasty, and couldn't believe that she'd had no inkling—not a thought—that her lovely cow had been in such a terrible way. She went behind the cow again and gripped the calf's legs to pull, but the mucus covering them made her hands slip. She found a handkerchief in her pocket, wrapped it around the cold wet shanks, pushed her foot against Spot's rump and heaved. The calf slid out a bit, but stopped at the hips. Spot moaned and Dusty pulled again, but now when she held the calf's forelegs she couldn't reach to put her foot against the cow. She'd lost her purchase. She heaved again, nothing. Again, no movement at all. She crawled forward and ran her fingers around the cow's vulva. It was loose; there was plenty of room. The calf's hips must be jammed deep inside her.

Dad, why aren't you here? she thought. I can't do this by myself. She gripped the bony legs again through the sodden hankie and heaved, but nothing budged. She was just about to race back to the house to get Rita when she saw a figure walking across the paddock, and a car parked on the road beyond. At first she thought it was Bill from up the road, who ran the newsagency in town and always went to work early. She cursed him for stopping, the busybody. He'd spend the rest of the week telling the town how badly the Rileys managed their farm. "Oh yes, and if I hadn't turned up when I did, blah, blah, blah . . ." But she suddenly realised that it was Barney—Barney with a rope.

He knelt beside her and without a word—with just a pat on the shoulder—he fastened the rope around the calf's legs and they pulled steadily together until it came away from the cow in a slippery rush of mucus and afterbirth. Then the words came tumbling out of Dusty in a torrent of recrimination and guilt.

"I knew I should have checked her again before I went to bed. I saw her after tea, but then I went to sleep." She looked closer at the calf and started to cry. "It was a male, a beautiful big boy."

Barney helped her to her feet and patted her shoulder again. "Well, Dusty, you can blame yourself as much as you like, but you know what? Shit happens."

When Jack came home he looked like a ghost and didn't even seem to hear when Dusty told him about Spot's calf.

"Why is he so useless?" Dusty asked Rita. "He's not helping at all."

It had taken Dusty ages to walk Spot to the yards, she was so weak and partly paralysed from the prolonged labour. Rita had rung Milo that morning and he had a two-day-old calf they could foster on to the cow. They skinned the dead calf and tied its hide on to the new calf, so Spot would recognise her own smell. She wasn't fooled, and kicked at the calf every time he went to drink. Her udder was huge and swollen and her teats looked tender.

Rita shoved the calf back in under the cow and ducked a kick. "It's the only way to make her feel better. Once he starts drinking it'll ease some of the pressure off her udder. We'll just have to be patient."

Dusty rubbed Spot on the bony top of her head. She loved that. "Why is Dad so sick, Mum? Other people don't look like that the morning after."

Rita sighed and leant her head against Spot's flank. "I don't think he should drink. He doesn't normally drink at all, as you know, but when he does, he keeps going until he falls over. He just can't stop himself."

11
Quicksilver

Dusty felt the Snow Pony rise like a bird and they cleared the first fence in a graceful arc. Air to spare, she thought to herself and looked on to the next jump. Her mother was always nagging her about focus. "Look there and you'll go there." She couldn't explain to Dusty why it worked, but it did. As you went over a jump, you looked on to the next one and the horse followed your eye.

This was the last show of the season, and the closest one to home, after Bankstown. Jack had driven her and Stewie today, so Rita could stay home and look after Spot and her calf. That's what she said, but Dusty thought it was just her way of getting Jack to spend some time with her and Stewie, of getting him off the farm. Dusty knew he would be watching, so she really wanted to win this jump-off. He hadn't seen her compete since the Bankstown Show last year, when the Snow Pony had disgraced herself, so it would be good for him to see how well she was going. The prize money was three hundred dollars for the win, and that would make him happy, too.

The Snow Pony galloped around the course. Dusty knew she was going too fast, and the "Teddy Bears' Picnic" was sounding like a chipmunk song, but sometimes she just had to let her go. She did everything fast. Sometimes Dusty felt as if she were riding greased lightning. Above the thunder of hooves and the mare's heavy breathing, Dusty could hear the jumps commentator on the loud-speaker system, old Johnny Ray, playing up to the crowd: "And here we have Dusty Riley, going like hell, as usual. What's the hurry, Dusty? Riding her brilliant young mare—caught on the high plains and broken by her father Jack—what he doesn't know about horses, ladies and gentlemen, wouldn't take long to write down at all . . . and Dusty's mother, Rita Poole that was, has done a beautiful job teaching her how to jump . . ."

The Snow Pony flew through the triple—jump stride, jump stride, jump. "Good girl." Dusty looked on to the next fence.

"So we have Dusty coming up now to the seventh fence, a brick wall, and she's over it beautifully. My word this mare can jump. And the kid can ride. I reckon this combination could do anything. If they go clear, they'll win this. No one's going to beat their time."

Only five jumps to go. "Come on, girl," Dusty breathed. "We can do this."

They were going so fast, Dusty's eyes were watering and the commentator was silent at the microphone. Over the picket fence, then over the oxer. The tenth jump was beside the oxer, so Dusty had to do a U-turn to approach it. She pushed the mare towards the edge of the arena, looked back over her shoulder, and the Snow Pony followed her eyes in a scorching turn, leaning so far in that Dusty felt as if she might brush her shoulder against the ground. She heard a gasp from the crowd as they anticipated a fall, but the mare kept her feet.

Over number eleven—easy—and on to the last jump, a set of blue-and-white rails on the far edge of the arena. The cypress trees hung over the fence, shading the jump, so Dusty concentrated. It was easy to muck up the last jump, but the Snow Pony flew over the blue rails. She landed clear, but suddenly, from the corner of her eye, Dusty saw an ugly yellow dog racing towards her. Snow saw it, too, and shied away in a massive leap that took her over the arena fence. Dusty saw a flash of frightened faces as the crowd parted, then she was fighting for control as the mare moved between her legs like quicksilver. She let her go, once they were through the crowd, and ended up cantering down the road behind the showgrounds. Tall gums grew on both sides of the road and dappled the sandy gravel with shade. The Snow Pony slowed to a walk and Dusty dropped the reins on her neck, pulled off her riding helmet and rubbed her hands through her hair. She couldn't bear to face her father.

She was eliminated, twice: once for leaving the arena and once for not passing the finish flags. There was no three hundred dollars.

∾

Dusty sat in the shade of the truck, leaning against a back wheel, and watched the line of cars, floats, and trucks stringing out of the showgrounds. The Snow Pony and Tarzan stood dozing quietly, washed and ready to load. Stew's day hadn't been much better than Dusty's. Second place in the bending race wasn't enough prize money to cover his entry fees. The loudspeaker was finally silent and scraps of litter danced through the dust in the low afternoon light as the carnival people dismantled their sideshows and rides. The drama of the day was over and the showgrounds were turning back to an oval of sunburnt grass surrounded by sad old cypress trees.

"Is he coming?" Stew called from the cab of the truck. He was lying on the seat, pretending to catnap, but Dusty knew his mind was racing as fast as hers, worrying and wrangling about how they were going to manage Dad when he got back to the truck, roaring drunk. He had to be drunk—he'd been over at the bar for four hours now.

The bar looked like one of those ads for beer they showed on TV, thought Dusty. It was a rectangular structure with no walls, just the roof and the bar. The men leaning against it were golden from the evening sun shining through the ghost gums. In their stockman's hats, moleskin trousers, and riding boots, they were the romantic image of true blue Aussies. Dusty wondered if all their kids were as miserable as she felt.

When she and Stew had gone over to see when they'd be going home, they'd ended up not even asking their dad, he looked like such a stranger. He was drinking with blokes from the town whom he wouldn't normally give the time of day. Drinking, bragging, big mouths—"cowboys" he'd scornfully described them once to Dusty—always skiting about the horses they'd ridden and the brumbies they'd driven. As they roared and raised their unsteady glasses to his story, Jack's swimming vision focused for a moment on his children standing on the edge of the crowd, but he looked straight through them and turned away.

It was nearly dark now, and there were only a few staggering figures left at the bar. The barman had packed up his kegs long ago and Dusty could see the men passing a bottle between them. The headlights of a car swung into the showgrounds and flashed past the bar before pulling in beside the truck. It was Mum.

"Get those horses on to the truck." She looked wild, her mouth set in a tight little line and her red hair sticking out as though she'd poked her finger in the toaster. "Come on, lead them up the ramp." She ruffled Stewie's hair as he led his pony past her and gave Dusty a thin smile.

Dusty wound up the ramp and peered across at the bar. Jack was standing with his back to them. "How's Dad going to get home? You can't leave the car for him. He'll crash."

Rita took the keys out of the car's ignition, slammed the door, and locked it. "I'm leaving him nothing. The dog can get his mates to look after him." Her voice was cracked and angry, but she didn't cry. "Come on, let's go home." As the truck rumbled past the bar she looked straight ahead, didn't even glance sideways. Jack kept his back to them, too, and Dusty felt as though she and Stewie were falling into a great chasm of loneliness between their fighting parents.

"Does this mean you and Dad are going to get divorced?" asked Stew in a tiny voice.

Then Rita did cry and Dusty cried too, and they drove down the long black road towards home.

12

The Morning After

A horrible sound woke Dusty. Someone was vomiting in the bathroom. Her heart sank as she remembered last night: the sound of a car outside, a door slamming, her father bursting into the lounge room, swaying in the doorway, glaring like a lunatic, and then launching into an insane tirade of bitterness against her and Mum and Stewie. Rita hadn't even tried to argue with him; she'd just turned on the television and taken herself and Stew and Dusty off to bed. They listened to him rampaging around the house until he finally fell into his favourite chair and began to snore, as the TV's numbing spell put him to sleep.

Now the morning had come and he was over his drunken rage, Rita got stuck into him. Dusty and Stew stayed in bed, out of the way. They could hear her voice, calm and level, as she stood in the doorway of the bathroom.

"I'm not going to put up with this. This marriage is over unless you swear to me now that you will never treat me and the kids like that again. There may be some women around here who'll wait while their husbands drink themselves rotten, but I'm not one of them."

Jack mumbled something Dusty couldn't understand, but it sent Rita into a rage.

"I don't care! Other people have hard times without turning into losers! You've got so much, you've always had so much—education, opportunity, a good family. Some people make their lives from nothing!"

More strangled retching sounds filtered through the wall.

"You disgust me."

Dusty heard her father moan. "Please, Rita. Not now. Leave me alone." His footsteps crossed the bathroom and then came the sound of the door shutting and the key turning in the lock.

"We should leave you alone for good, you dog," Rita muttered as she walked away.

Dusty listened for noises from the bathroom; clues of what he was up to. She could hear him going through the shelves in the bathroom cupboard, looking through the pills. The terrible words of that other fight suddenly came into her head. "You'd be happy if I blew my brains out." Maybe he was going to take an overdose. Muffled sobs came from under Stewie's doona, and Dusty knew he was thinking the same thing.

She jumped out of bed, raced to the bathroom, and pounded on the door. "Are you all right, Dad? Come out! Dad! Answer me!" There was no answer. Dusty turned the doorknob and pushed against the door with all her might, but it didn't budge. She raced down the passage to the kitchen, skidding on the lino in her socks. "Mum! What if he kills himself?"

Rita was chopping up a pumpkin with the big butcher's

knife, banging the blade through the orange flesh with both hands. It was hard work and she was breathing heavily. She looked up at Dusty and the air around her crackled with anger. "He won't." She thudded the knife into the flesh again. "He's too gutless!" She kept chopping maniacally, shaving off the hard shell and tossing orange chunks into the big enamel soup saucepan. After a little while she looked up and saw Dusty's eyes swimming with tears and her face softened.

"Sweetie." She held her arms out so Dusty could walk into them. "He'll be all right. He's an adult. He just has to work it out." Rita kissed her daughter's hair, still in yesterday's ponytail. "I'm not going to bash down the bathroom door to get to him."

"Then I'll go and watch him from outside," said Dusty. "You can see right into the bathroom from the tulip tree." She gently untangled herself from her mother and pushed the back door open.

Mum turned and started to attack the pumpkin again.

"You don't have to look after him, you know," Rita called as she crossed the dewy lawn in her socks. "You're a kid. He's supposed to be looking after you."

Stewie came and joined her in their tree. One day last year, when they were in the tree, the Avon lady had come into the bathroom and settled on the toilet like an old chook. They had squirmed and wriggled so much then, trying not to laugh out loud, that they had nearly fallen, but today they sat as still as sentinels, watching over their shamed father as he sat with his head in his hands.

❧

They sat around the kitchen table like polite strangers,

talking only to offer salt and pepper, or tomato sauce. Dusty felt as though she'd been rubbed all over with sandpaper, her emotions were so raw.

Rita rose to clear the dinner plates away but Jack motioned her to sit. "I'll do it."

That's a start, thought Dusty. Normally he'd make her or Stewie do it. He carried the plates over to the sink and rinsed them, then walked past the table where his family was sitting, waiting. He stood at the window looking out at nothing, and his hand came up to the back of his head, the way it always did when he was about to make a speech.

"First, I've got to apologise. I've been a fair mongrel to all of you lately and I've nearly lost you." He turned to them and his eyes were the same pale blue as the evening sky behind him. "I'll never get your respect back altogether, but I promise I'm not going to drink again. I know a promise is nothing if you don't keep it, but I'm going to. I've been so hung up about keeping this place, I've lost sight of everything else. But it'd mean nothing if I didn't have you three."

His eyes dropped to the floor and no one spoke, though Dusty knew Stewie was thinking the same thing as she was. Finally she blurted it out. "We just want you to stop being a pig."

Rita snorted in surprise.

"Sorry, Mum, but you know what I mean. He's not just horrible when he's drunk. He's mean to us all the time."

"Yeah." Stewie plucked up courage and had his say as well. "And grumpy."

"They're right, Jack, and you're right, too. Talk is

84

cheap. You have to make that phone call we've talked about. You have to ring up and ask for help, admit that you're not perfect." Rita reached over the back of her chair, grabbed the bottom of his jumper, and pulled him from his lonely place on the lino into their circle at the table. "Times are tough, but we live in a beautiful place, and we're all well. Be happy."

Her words were bold and optimistic, and they all knew it wasn't that easy.

"What we need to talk about," she said, "is the muster—bringing our cattle down from the high plains."

∾

Dusty reached into the linen cupboard for a clean towel and froze as she heard the phone dialling out. Ring ring, ring ring. Somebody picked up at the other end, and her father cleared his throat. "Is that the Drug and Alcohol Help Line? My name is Jack Riley. I'm after some help."

Good on you, thought Dusty, come right out and say it.

"No, it's not for someone else. It's me with the problem."

Dusty listened, staring into the dark shelves of towels, sheets, and tablecloths, as Jack wrote down meeting times and addresses, and she found her eyes filling with tears. When he stepped into the passage she grabbed him in a fierce bear hug, and whispered against his chest, "Good on you, Dad."

He hugged her back. "Well it's a start. Like your mother says, you have to admit you have a problem before you can fix it."

Dusty shut the cupboard and they walked down the passage to join Rita and Stewie in front of the fire.

85

PART TWO

13

The Shooting Party

Jade peered out of the dirty windscreen as the overloaded Toyota roared towards the mountains, and wondered if they would ever slow down enough to see anything.

"We'll never see a deer going this fast," she thought aloud, and that sent Horse into gales of wheezy laughter. His breath was so vile it made her stomach heave.

"Chicks! You don't know nothin', do yah? Travis, this sister of yours knows nothin'. The deer aren't here, ya little bird brain, they're up the top, up on the high plains, up in man's country." He growled out the last two words, banged his fat paw of a hand down on Jade's skinny thigh, and gave it a squeeze. "Man's country! A little sheila like you could get into all sorts of trouble up there." He sniggered more foul air into the cabin.

Jade looked down at the fingers resting on her leg like hairy sausages about to burst on the barbie, and shoved them aside. "Nick off, Horse!" she growled, hoping her voice wouldn't betray her fear, because that's what she suddenly felt.

She felt sick that a slob like Horse would come on to her. She was only a kid, only fifteen, and he was nearly thirty. He'd always given her the creeps, ever since Travis started doing his apprenticeship with him. Their dad had left the year before, and Horse saw himself as the man about the house they had to have.

"He's been very good to us, Jade," Jeannie ticked her off when she complained about him hanging around like a bad smell. "He can't help the way he looks."

Jade knew that her mum and Trav put up with Horse because he was useful to them. He chopped all the firewood for Mum and put the rubbish bins out, and he did give Trav a lot of things he'd have missed out on otherwise: took him to footy, taught him to shoot. Horse looked up to Jeannie—he worshipped the ground she walked on—but now that they were away from home and Jeannie wasn't there to see, Jade felt as if he had her in his sights, like a frightened rabbit.

She banged her thigh against Trav's and stared at the side of his head, wanting to catch his eye so that she could signal to him: "Do something. Tell him to pull his head in. Tell him to knock it off. Say something." But Travis wouldn't meet her gaze. He stared hard out the window, not turning even when she elbowed him. His pinched mouth gave him away. He's just as scared as I am, thought Jade. Scared of Horse and probably scared of Neville, as well. In the truck, with a beer between his legs and the back full of guns and dogs, Horse wasn't such a joke any more.

Jade hadn't met Neville before yesterday, and she didn't think her brother had either. He was just a bit older than Horse, Jade thought, but she wasn't sure because Neville had hardly spoken all day, just packed his guns into the

89

racks behind the front seats, loaded up his dogs, given her a hard look—up and down with his icy blue eyes—then crawled on to the back seat and gone to sleep.

"He's a top hunter," Horse told them. "Knows his guns, knows his dogs, knows the mountains. Just don't get him drinking rum. He goes feral on it."

∾

Maybe wagging school this week wasn't such a great idea after all, thought Jade. On Monday morning, it had made sense. Mum had come into her room on Sunday night and kissed her goodbye.

"I've got to go to Melbourne, love. Shazz wants me to look after the twins while she runs another astrology workshop. I can get a lift if I go tonight. Travis will be . . ."

"When are you coming back?" Jade's voice was muffled under the doona. If she sat up she'd probably start howling. She hated her mother going away, but she was always doing it.

"I'll be back on Thursday night. That's okay, isn't it? You'll have a groovy time with Trav. He'll be here. You can have take-away every night." She lay on the bed beside Jade and nestled her long skinny body up against her, then lifted the doona and kissed her on the neck. "I love you, Jadey, my beautiful girl, my big girl."

Jade didn't feel like a big girl, she felt like a teeny tiny little girl, alone and afraid, but there was no point saying anything. Her mum always ended up doing what she wanted, always got Jade to see her point of view, but she had no idea how awful this house was when she wasn't here. When Jeannie was home there was always music playing—loud music—there was food cooking, incense burning, crystals glinting, and always something being made, maybe to sell, maybe for them: sewing, painting, candles, jewellery. It was a house of fun. When she was gone, it was so quiet and empty. Suddenly you noticed the shabby carpet, different in every room, and the broken windows patched with rainbow transfers, plastic, and masking tape. There was never any decent food. Travis just watched TV and never cooked anything or even made a cup of tea. When Jade woke in the mornings he was already gone, picked up by Horse at six-thirty. It was horrible getting up by yourself and having breakfast alone. Kayfer used to keep her company, but he had been skittled on the highway last Christmas and Mum wouldn't get another cat.

Jeannie stood up with a yawn and leant over to ruffle Jade's silky blonde hair. "You'll be right, won't you, Jadey? I'll buy you something cool in the city. You'll be right. Goodnight now."

She rocked Jade's shoulder gently, signalling her to answer, and even though Jade could feel her heart shrinking like a cold little stone inside her, she managed to lie. "Sure, I'll be fine, Mum. Goodnight. Have fun in Melbourne." And that's the truth, she thought as her mother rustled out of the room. She was going to have fun. She could easily look after the twins here while Auntie Shazz did her stupid star readings, but she wanted to be away, to be in Melbourne, to go *out*. Jade had heard her joking on the phone, "Yeah, we're gunna party hard, sister. Go hard or go home, ha ha ha."

A part of Jade wished Jeannie was more like one of

those fat mums other kids had; the ones who always did reading at school when she was little, worked in the canteen, baked cakes for birthdays, and never went away. The other part loved her for being the way she was: wild and funny and beautiful. The first time she'd picked Jade up from high school, even the year twelves were asking the next day who she was. She looked like a rock star with her long dreadlocks that changed colour every week, and silver and turquoise jewellery on every ear, arm, finger, and toe. It was as if a famous band had passed through the town one night and she had been left behind. In fact she had come to live in Bankstown when Jade's dad had got work on the oil rigs, and when he left, there didn't seem to be any point in her leaving. The kids were settled in school and she could never afford a house in Melbourne. "As long as I can get away every now and again," Jade heard her telling her sister on the phone, "and get a bit of action, I'll be cool. It's dull here, but it's peaceful, too."

Jeannie had only been gone for about an hour on Sunday night when the telephone rang, crashing through the TV's dull noise like an intruder. Trav's voice rose enthusiastically as the conversation developed, and then Jade heard it drop with disappointment.

"Damn! I just remembered. I've got to stay here with Jade. Mum's gone to Melbourne. Bummer!" Jade listened, mumble, mumble . . . "Hang on. I'll go and ask her." Boom, boom, boom, he thumped down the passage. Dad used to say Travis walked as if he were trying to poke holes in the floor.

"You awake, Jadey?" He was standing in the doorway.

"Mmmnn. What is it?"

"It's Horse. He's got a mate down from Bendigo and they're going up to the high plains tomorrow to hunt deer."

"So what?"

"So he wants to know if I want to go too."

Jade felt the tears creeping back into her eyes. "No way. I'm not staying here by myself. And I'm not asking Natalie if I can stay at her place. I always feel like such a—"

"I'm not asking you to do that." Travis slid to and fro across the lino in his socks, holding the portable phone like a laser gun. His silhouette looked excited. "Horse says you can come, too. Do ya wanna wag school for the week?"

14
Heading for the Hills

Just like the old days, thought Dusty—Dad and Stewie and me heading up to the high plains, horses in the back of the truck, dogs in the dog box, food and gear behind the seat, missing school for a week. It felt strange leaving Mum behind—she'd always come with them—but she had to stay at home this time because some new potential showjumpers were arriving.

"I need to make sure that cow of yours feeds her calf, too," she said to Dusty as they packed gear for the trip together in the laundry. "You might have to be the strong one on this trip." She looked up and peered into Dusty's face. "Do you know what I mean?"

Dusty nodded and a squeeze of panic passed through her.

Rita sighed. "He says he's okay and I hope he is, but I'm not convinced. If he falls to pieces, I don't know what you're going to do."

Dusty patted her mum's shoulder. "We'll be right, Mum. He loves the plains. It'll do him good to get up there."

"And you know I'm not happy about you taking the

Snow Pony. She's wild enough down here. She might go completely crazy when she's back on her home ground."

This would be the first time the Snow Pony had been back to the high plains since Jack first brought her down, tethered to Chester. Jack and Rita both wanted to leave her behind, but Dusty had refused point blank and they were so desperate to maintain the fragile peace in the family that they had given in. Spook was so old he was nearly worn out, and Dusty longed to ride her wild horse in her own wild country. But at the same time, a little niggling voice in her head said, "What if she wants to stay there? What if that's her real home. What will you do then?"

The truck groaned up the hills.

"I don't like the look of this sky," Jack said, changing gears again. "We've never left the cattle this late." Dusty had heard her parents arguing for the last month about bringing the cattle down. All their cows were on the high plains, three hundred of them. There was plenty of feed in the mountains, Rita reasoned, and none at home, so it made sense to leave them up there. Jack agreed with her theory, but worried about the weather turning. He knew the high plains as well as anyone. The government deadline for cattle to be off the leased country was weeks ago, but in these tough times the rangers turned a blind eye. Rita had won the argument—as usual, Jack would say— and the cows had stayed on the plains for a while longer. The one time Dusty heard her dad laugh recently was when a joke came over the fax, saying: "For Sale, complete set of Encyclopaedia. No longer needed. Wife knows everything."

The truck groaned on. Dusty had forgotten how slow the trip was. She could have walked faster than the truck on this steep bit. "Mum's an optimist," she said. "She wants the weather to stay fine, so she thinks it will."

"Mmmnn." Jack looked hard at the road ahead. "Her father used to say she was pig-headed, but perhaps it means the same thing. Anyway, whether we're snowed on or not, she's given the cows an extra two weeks of good feed. They won't know what's hit them when they get home and start living on starvation rations."

❧

"Look! The gate's open, Dad," said Stewie. "Maybe Fred's up here, too." They could see the padlock hanging on its chain.

"No," Jack shook his head and his voice was puzzled. "He's away droving, up in Queensland. And he wouldn't leave the gate open, anyway." He drove the truck through the gateway then stopped the engine and jumped out.

Stewie watched him in the side mirror. "He's looking at the chain. He's coming back. He's getting in the truck . . . What is it, Dad?"

Jack pulled a face as he started the engine. "Someone's cut the chain with bolt cutters. I hope they haven't cleaned us out."

They drove through the snow gums to the house, expecting to see the door smashed in or windows broken, but it seemed intact.

"The padlock's still on the shed," said Jack. "Let's get the horses unloaded, then we'll have a closer look."

Dusty and Stewie led the three horses across to the horse paddock and let them go. They trotted away,

96

propping playfully at imaginary snakes in the grass and shying away from each other. Dusty watched the Snow Pony carefully as she whinnied.

"Do you think she's calling Hillbilly?" asked Stewie. They watched the edge of the bush, expecting him to appear. "Where is he? He's always here to meet us."

"Hillbilly!" Dusty called out. "Hillbilly! Come up!" Her voice faded across the plain. Maybe he was in the trees and hadn't heard the truck.

They watched the horses break into a canter and race across the paddock. The Snow Pony didn't look as though she was going to race away, sticking close to the other horses. At the gully they pulled up short, snorting and staring down at something in it.

"He must be stuck in the creek, Stew."

They ran, stumbling through the tussocky snow grass, their hearts racing. The horses wheeled away like mad things as they got to the gully, and Dusty saw straight away why they were so upset. Hillbilly was dead, his legs sticking out stiffly, like a stuffed animal.

"Don't look, Stew!" Dusty pushed him away. "Go and get Dad." She didn't want Stew to see what she'd seen. Hillbilly's sweet old face was caked with dried blood and there was a bullet hole right between his eyes.

∾

The house and the shed were intact; nothing had been stolen. Jack shone his torch on the track as evening darkened around them, and from the wheel marks they guessed that the intruders had cut the chain, driven in and driven out again, touching nothing, just shooting Hillbilly.

Dusty was stunned by the stupidity of it.

"They probably didn't even know what they were shooting," Jack said. "They would have seen his eyes in their lights and just gone *boom*. You get some pretty dopey people up here shooting deer."

∾

It was dark by the time Jack unlocked the house and they got inside. Dusty lit the gas lanterns and the kitchen heater and looked around this house she knew so well. Her grandparents had lived here for a while when her dad was little, and her grandmother had given this kitchen the same treatment as the one at home, painting all the cupboards different colours.

Jack put the casserole Rita had made for them—lamb again—in the oven, then sat at the streaky red laminex table and rang the Banjo police. Tom Jackson's voice was so loud that Dusty and Stew could hear both sides of the conversation from the lounge room, where they were lighting the fire. Jack chatted for a while, then described what they had found at The Plains. The kids smirked at each other as Tom began to speak. He had the odd habit of grunting before he answered a question. Rita thought it was a nervous thing, but Jack said it was something he'd developed over the years to give himself time to think. Whatever the reason, his snort meant that everybody called him Grunter behind his back, which, as Rita pointed out, was an unfortunate name for a policeman.

Jack continued. "Anyway, Tom, I thought I should let you know. Have you had anyone causing trouble?"

Dusty looked at Stewie. He was nearly bursting with laughter. Here it came . . .

"Hmmnnff . . . Well, there was a group at the pub yesterday. They didn't exactly cause trouble but they looked like they could, if you know what I mean. Hmmnnf. Had some hounds and a stack of guns. Three blokes and a scraggy looking girl."

"Do you know where they were from?" interrupted Jack.

Dusty grinned; it was coming again.

"Hmmnnf. One was from way over the other side of Melbourne. A mean looking begger. The hounds belonged to him. I checked their gun licences and I wrote down all the details, Jack, so we'll be able to track them down. The girl looked right out of her depth. The younger bloke was her brother. Anyway, you look out for them because the two bigger ones were nasty types. Pity you haven't got a two-way you can call me on. I guess once you get out to the leases you'll be out of touch."

The fire started to catch and soon its crackling drowned out the conversation.

Dinner was delicious. Food always tasted good at The Plains. Dusty forgot how she hated lamb, and mopped up the rich brown gravy with bread. Dad made a cup of tea, and the three of them sat at the table and planned the next two days. Tomorrow they'd ride out to the hut and the holding yards that Jack's grandfather had built nearly a hundred years ago, and muster the cattle from there. They'd reach the hut before lunch, and muster all the south side of their lease that afternoon. After staying the night at the hut, they would muster the northern section in the morning, then bring the mob back to The Plains. The three days after that would be easy, droving the cows

99

down the road to home. Jack would trot his horse back and bring the truck to their camp each night. Dusty loved it when he did that, when she felt like she was in charge of the whole show.

Jack pushed back his chair and stretched. "We'll have a lot of packing in the morning, so you two better get off to bed."

Dusty and Stew rolled their swags out in the lounge and cleaned their teeth. Dusty changed into some tracksuit pants, but Stewie just climbed into bed in his clothes.

"You're so festy, Stew!"

"Don't you dare tell Dad. It's too cold," he explained. "And this way, I don't have to get dressed in the morning."

Their father came into the lounge and knelt between the beds, his shadow like a monster on the wall behind him. He kissed them both goodnight. "Thanks for your help, kids. It's been a sad day, but at least Hillbilly wouldn't have known what hit him. It would have been instant."

He went out to the kitchen and they could hear him sorting supplies and packing saddle bags. After a while he dialled out on the telephone and talked for a long while to Rita. Her voice didn't boom through the house like Tom Jackson's did, so they only caught one side of the conversation, but it seemed as though their parents were talking more than they had for months. After he hung up the phone, Jack went outside and the banging of doors told them he was getting something out of the truck. When he came back, Dusty strained her ears to work out what it was, but it was the smell of oil that told her as much as the metallic clicking and snapping.

He was cleaning the gun! Suddenly Dusty felt as if she were in a western with the bad guys at the door. The only thing she had ever been taught to fear at The Plains was the weather. It was their place, and no one was ever a danger here. She looked across at Stewie, but he was asleep, so she crawled out of her swag and padded out to the kitchen. Jack was holding the shotgun up, checking the barrels. The gun made him look wild and dangerous. She stood in the doorway, blinking in the light.

"Dad! D'you think they might come back?"

He laid the open gun gently on the table and held out his arm so she could sit on his knee, then rested the side of his head against her back. "No, I'm sure they won't. They'll be miles away, chasing some poor deer."

"Poor dear," joked Dusty. "Ha ha."

"No, I'm not worried about them," Jack went on smiling at her feeble joke. "If they'd been real mongrels they'd have smashed this place up. They just made a dumb mistake. And I think a gun would only get us into strife if they did come back. It's always better to talk your way out of trouble. No, it was your mum. She made me promise I'd sleep with the gun in the house."

Dusty padded back to bed and shivered in her sleeping-bag, waiting for the downy cover to warm her up again. The image of her father with the raised shotgun stuck in her mind, and she realised that if she'd seen him like that two days ago she would have thought he was about to harm himself, but tonight it hadn't crossed her mind. Things had changed.

∽

When Dusty woke in the morning it was as though the

101

night had passed in a moment. It felt just the same as coming out of the anaesthetic, when they'd stitched her cheek. One minute she was counting to ten, next minute the nurse was waking her up, and it seemed impossible that the operation could have occurred in such a short time.

"Come on you two—up!" Jack called from the kitchen. "I've already caught your horses and saddled them."

The outside door banged as he carried gear out to the verandah. Stewie groaned and climbed out of his sleeping-bag. His ginger hair always stuck out at crazy angles when he got up, and this morning it was wilder than ever.

"See," he stood in his rumpled clothes and smiled sleepily at Dusty, "ready for action. No cold bits for this little brown duck."

Dusty laughed. "You look more like a cocky than a duck. Have a look in the mirror." She shivered as she changed into her moleskins and pulled her bra up under her shirt. It was freezing.

They ate their porridge like sleepy owls, blinking in the kitchen light and not speaking as Jack banged in and out of the house, sorting and packing. Dusty waited for the tension to rise, as it often did when her father was trying to get something done by a certain time, but he stayed determinedly cheerful, just chipping them now and again: "Come on eat up, get your sleeping-bags rolled up, no you can't take a pillow, Stew, I think you should wear your oil-skin coats, you'll need hats and gloves, too."

Even when Stewie brought his sleeping-bag out to be loaded, rolled into a hopeless, floppy sausage that would unravel within an hour, Jack didn't lose his cool. "Bring it over here, mate, and we'll roll it up again. That's right, spread it out on the verandah."

The only one who got yelled at was Spike, when he walked on the sleeping-bag with his muddy paws.

As Dusty cleaned her teeth, she looked at her reflection in the tarnished mirror that hung over the basin and raised an eyebrow, as if to say, "How's he going?" and her reflection grinned wryly, nodding back, "He's going all right."

15
Mustering

"Remember the time Captain bolted here with you, Stewie?" asked Jack, as they rode on to the first big plain beyond the house. Streaks of red showed through sullen clouds in the eastern sky and a biting wind sliced around them. It was just light enough to see, and the snow gums circling the plain stood out like ghosts in the morning gloom. Stew laughed at the memory of the day. He'd been seven years old. Rita had been riding a young horse she was educating, so she had let Stewie ride Captain. It was his first time on a big horse, and when they began to canter the unfamiliar movement of Captain's long stride gave him a fright, so he gripped hard with his legs. The trouble was, he'd forgotten he was wearing spurs, and the tighter he clung, the more he poked the spurs into the horse's sides.

Captain took off like a rocket and kept going. The rest of the family reined in their horses and sat gaping at the big bay flash-circling the plain. They had never seen Captain move so fast. Finally they'd realised what was making him bolt and they'd started yelling at Stew, every time his circuit brought him close enough to hear: "Stick your feet out! Stop gripping him with your heels! Pull the spurs out of him!"

Afterwards Stewie said the wind was rushing so loudly in his ears he couldn't hear anything. But he must have stopped spurring the poor horse because eventually Captain flew up to the other horses and halted with such a sudden prop that Stewie sailed straight over his head, did a somersault in midair, and landed on his feet. It was the most amazing thing Dusty had ever seen. Jack got off his horse and walked across to his shaken son. "I think we'd better take those spurs off, mate," he had said, and Dusty and her mum just howled with laughter.

They rode on in silence, following the bridle path that generations of riders had used before them, winding through the snow gums, crossing another plain and slipping into the trees again. They had too much gear tied to their saddles to go any faster than a walk: food, oats for the horses, the bag of shoeing gear, woollen horse rugs, two billies, their sleeping bags bundled in plastic, and bags of salt for the cattle, all bumped and rattled as the horses stepped out. After a summer on the high plains the cattle craved salt, and would come running for it when they heard the call, "Saaaalt!"

The Snow Pony's ears were pricked, but she felt relaxed and easy, almost as if she were thinking, oh, this, yes, I remember this. After plodding along on Spook for the last two trips, Dusty felt as if she were floating through the country on her beautiful, free-moving horse.

The bridle path wound across the plains and by mid-morning it had brought them to the four-wheel-drive track that ran out to their hut from the Mountain Road.

"Whoa!" Jack reined in his horse and leant over the salt and saddle bags tied to the front of his saddle, peering down at the track.

"What can you see, Dad? Have they come out here?" Dusty had been worrying all morning that the shooters might be at their hut. It wasn't really *their* hut. The Rileys had built and maintained it, but it was on crown land and, like all the huts on the high plains, it was open to anyone who needed shelter.

Jack turned his horse and rode a little way along the track, all the time leaning and searching for tracks. "No, I think we're in luck. There hasn't been a vehicle along here for weeks."

As they rode down into the clearing, the clouds parted for a moment and a shaft of sunlight played on the hut like a spotlight through the mist. Dusty's heart skipped a beat to see it, sitting in front of the gnarled trees like a little cat, with the silvered rails of the yards spread behind. The shingles of the original roof had been covered with corrugated iron many years ago and the tin, pitched steeply so that snow would slide off it, was dented and rusty. The walls were made of logs, silver with age and chocked on top of each other, and the chimney, built on the end of the hut, was corrugated iron too, with an exterior framework of wooden poles and a stone base.

A sagging verandah had been tacked on to the front of the hut and it made the two tiny windows look as though they were peeping from under a battered felt hat. Firewood was stacked under the windows, the sawn ends of the logs round and orange. At the end of the verandah were the dog kennels—two ancient hollow logs, silver and lichen-covered.

Dusty hooked Snow's reins on to a piece of rusty wire hanging off the verandah rail, and ran to the door. She poked her hand through a tiny hole carved in it and felt for the string, up and to the right, where she knew it would be. She pulled, and the door swung open with a creak.

It was dark and very still inside. The only things moving were tiny motes of dust swirling through the shafts of light angling down from the windows. Dusty's riding boots sounded hollow on the uneven slab floor. Everything was the same: the bunks, made of curving snow gum branches worn smooth by decades of sleepy-heads climbing in and out of them, held lumpy ticking mattresses; the mouse-proof cupboard still leant a bit to one side where the milo tin replacing the missing leg wasn't quite big enough. The fireplace was huge, with a cast iron frame that swung around to support the camp oven, griddle pan, and billy over the open fire. A pile of wood—a mixture of dry leaves, twigs, branches, and logs—was stacked beside the fireplace, left by the last person to stay in the hut. It was an unwritten rule on the high plains that after you stayed at a hut you left enough wood for the next person to start their fire. Many a rider or bushwalker had been glad of that consideration over the years, when they stumbled, cold and exhausted, into a hut after hours of slogging through a blizzard. The poles and rafters in the hut were scarred with names and dates, burnt into them with the red-hot poker on countless flickering firelit nights by visitors leaving their mark.

The chinks between the logs were stuffed with mud, sphagnum moss, and newspaper to keep the draughts out. Last autumn, Dusty had pulled a wedge of wadded newspaper out of a crack and carefully laid out the pieces that fell apart as she unfolded it. Jack and Rita and Stewie had leant over her shoulders and pieced together the date and stories from the fragments.

"Wednesday the twenty-eighth of May, nineteen twenty-three. That's seventy-four years ago!" Rita was always quick at sums.

"You and Dad weren't even born then," said Stewie slowly. They squinted in the candle light to read the tiny print.

"Look! It says something about a drought in Banjo." Dusty held a tiny fragment steady with her finger. "And here's another story about the high plains. The snow came early and everyone got caught with their cattle up here. No, horses . . . two hundred and fifty horses. Why did they have such a big mob of horses?" She smiled to think what a fine sight that many horses would make, galloping through the snow.

"Your grandparents ran horses up here for a while, too," Jack told her, "but they'd stopped a few years before that storm. Back then, everyone needed a horse. Once the motor car came out, there wasn't the demand for horses, so they switched over to cattle. But they used to breed horses for the Indian army, too, and crossbred horses like Captain—Clydesdale thoroughbred crosses. Clumpers, they called them. They bred them, broke them, ran them

108

up here, then sold them. That generation were wonderful horsemen."

"And horsewomen," Rita added. "Your Auntie Bess broke in a heap of those horses. She used to tie one of the horse's back legs up with a strap and hop on." She turned to Dusty. "Remember Great Auntie Bess? You came with me to see her in hospital when you were little."

Dusty remembered the tiny woman, frail and trembling in her pink nightie. It was hard to imagine her bouncing around the yards on a big bucking Captain.

Jack leant on the mantelpiece, gazing down into the flames, lost in the past. "I can remember Dad telling me about that time. He was just a kid then and they were up here mustering and got caught by the early snow, too. He had a big strong mare and she plunged through the snow drifts and made a path and the cattle followed. His brother, your Great Uncle Harry, was at the back of the mob and he said it was like riding through a canyon, the walls of the channel they made in the snow were so high."

They had talked for hours that night, and Dusty and Stewie soaked up the stories about their family and the old days on the high plains. Dusty looked around the hut and hoped they'd talk like that again tonight.

"Hey! Lost in space?" Jack stepped sideways through the doorway, his arms full, and dropped a saddlebag on the table. "Make the sandwiches while Stewie and I get this gear unpacked."

Dusty undid the buckles on the leather bag. Everything she needed was there: a newspaper that she unfolded and spread out as a tablecloth, a solid chunk of corned beef, wrapped in silver foil, a pocket knife, a loaf of sourdough bread, and a jar of Rita's relish. She cut and spread, and soon had three mighty sandwiches ready, the bread as thick as doorsteps. There was no time for a cup of tea, but they each had fruit juice in a box. Stewie set the fire and brought a billy of water from the plastic pipe that fed down from the spring, and Jack put everything away. When they got back to the hut it would be late in the day, so it was good to have everything ready.

∾

They rode away from the hut, following the track to the southern lease. The wind had dropped and the horses strode out, happy to be free of the bags and bundles that had bumped on them all morning. Dusty and Stewie dropped the reins on their horses' necks and peeled a mandarin each before they put their gloves on, throwing bits of peel at their father as he rode ahead of them, trying to land a piece in the brim of his hat. Digger padded faithfully at Drover's heels and Spike, the young dog, tail waving like a banner, weaved excitedly up and down the track between the horses. Every now and then they had to detour through the bush, winding between trees and ducking under branches because a tree had fallen over the track. Dusty jumped most of the fallen trees, trotting up first and checking that the far side of the log was clear for landing, then taking the Snow Pony back and cantering in to fly over it.

"She might as well have wings," Jack said to Stewie as they bashed through the bush.

This is what a fish must feel like in water, thought

110

Dusty. The Snow Pony felt totally at home in this place.

The small clearings they rode through were carpeted with clover—lush green feed that had thrived on the high plains since it was introduced by cattlemen many years ago. Captain swiped mouthfuls of it as he walked along, ignoring Stewie's kicking.

"There's usually cattle up here." Jack looked anxiously up at the sky through the tree tops. "I really don't like the look of this sky. It feels like snow. And that would explain why the cattle aren't here. They're down in the gullies, sheltering." He turned to Dusty. "You can feel it, can't you? The atmosphere actually feels different. They say the creeks rise just before a big break in the weather."

When they reached the bottom plain they saw that Jack was right. Nearly fifty cows were grazing there with their calves, and when Jack put out salt and called, another forty odd came bellowing and bawling out of the trees. Stewie stayed on the plain, riding around the edges and turning back any cows that tried to stray back into the bush, while Dusty and Jack cantered further down the track to search the sheltered gullies that they knew the cattle loved.

Dusty remembered the muster last autumn, when she had ridden down here on Spook with Rita, looking for cattle, and they'd found the area devastated. Wild winds had swept along the side of the valley, bringing down trees and branches. At first the horses panicked in the crisscross of logs, and Rita was worried that they would fall. The horses had to wriggle through tiny gaps between trees, jump over logs from a standstill, slide down banks, and scramble through fallen branches. In one tree-choked

111

gully the smell of death made the horses spook and snort. Rita left Dusty holding them and climbed through the branches to find the rotting bodies of four cows. The storm had brought trees crashing down around them in an impenetrable tangle, imprisoning the poor beasts. They had died of thirst, their calves with them. In the end they were fifteen short in their count, so they reckoned the same thing had happened in other places.

∾

By three o'clock Dusty and Jack had found another twenty cows, scattered in small groups along the valley, and herded them back up the track to the bottom plain to join Stewie and the big mob. They called as they went so that any cows further out would hear and follow them to the hut. It was not unusual to wake at the hut on the second day and find cows standing patiently at the slip rails, waiting to join the mob in the yards.

When they got back to Stewie and the main mob, Dusty rode the Snow Pony back along the track, heading for the hut, and called the cows to follow her. "Come on, old girls, come on, come on." Jack stayed beside the track where it led up from the plain, to count the cows as they passed, and Stewie and the dogs hunted them off the grassy flats.

It was hard work because the cows didn't want to leave. Usually they were happy to begin the journey home, but not today. They ducked and dodged and cut back and even bailed up the dogs as Stewie raced up and down on Captain, cracking his stockwhip and shouting at them to move. Jack finally abandoned his counting position and rode back to help. Stew's language was getting worse and worse as his frustration grew. Even Captain got sick of the cattle being so stubborn and snaked his head forward to bite the slow ones on the bum with his big yellow teeth.

Finally they had them on the track heading to the hut, but it was a difficult journey with cows constantly trying to sneak into the bush and dogs and riders turning them back. Jack nearly blew his socks off yelling at Spike, who seemed to be in the wrong place all the time. Finally he got off Drover and called Spike. Stewie was frightened he was going to hurt the young dog, but he just strapped one of Spike's front paws into his collar and got back on his horse.

"He's got too much energy," he called in answer to Stewie's puzzled stare. "If he has to run on three legs for a while it will slow him down, and he'll stop being stupid."

Dusty rode at the front of the mob, stretching her legs out of the stirrups and wriggling her toes to try to warm up her feet. The Snow Pony had gone like a dream all day. It was very cold and still, and the sky looked dirty through the trees. She could hear from the yelling and whip-cracking behind her that Jack and Stewie were having a difficult time, and she felt glad that she was riding in the lead. Suddenly the Snow Pony stopped dead, head up and looking straight ahead. Dusty patted her shoulder.

"What's wrong, girl?"

The mare was trembling and tense. She felt as if she might turn and run in a split second. Then Dusty heard it, above the noise of dogs and whips and shouting—a sharp crack that came down through the trees from the direction of the hut. She listened, and there it was again. It seemed as though someone was answering the sound of Jack and Stewie's whips, but it wasn't a whip making that noise. It was a much sharper crack—louder and harder. It was the crack of a gun.

16
The Showdown

Dusty wanted to turn the cows and ride back to her father, but the leaders knew where they were going now and no amount of shouting would turn them back. They pushed up behind the Snow Pony, who pranced and side-stepped like a dervish, suddenly in a lather of sweat, forcing her towards the hut. Dusty knew it had to be the hunters at the hut, but she couldn't get back to tell her father. The cows were strung out along the track for almost a kilometre. She could never battle past them, or get through the bush in time.

She looked at the front cows, old Curly Horn and Red Eye leading the mob as usual, and she knew she couldn't abandon them. They were plodding on determinedly, unperturbed by the shots or the panicking horse in front of them. If the shooters were the same people who had shot Hillbilly, they wouldn't hesitate to shoot a cow.

The shots were louder as Dusty got closer to the hut and she started to shout and cooee, hoping they would hear her calls and stop shooting. They didn't, but the combination of shouting and being shaken to bits on her panicked horse made Dusty wild. When she was little,

Rita used to tell her to growl at her pony when he misbehaved. "He'll know you're cross with him, and a big voice will always make you feel much braver, too." It worked. By the time the Snow Pony danced around the final turn before the hut, Dusty was furious. "Stop it!" she screamed, "Stop shooting those bloody guns!"

The shooting did stop, but when Dusty looked around the clearing in front of the hut, her anger turned to fear. The gunman lounged on the bonnet of a battered troop carrier that sat crookedly outside the hut. He was a big dirty man, dressed in typical hunter's clothes: plaid shirt, beanie, jeans, and boots. He swung a bottle of whisky in one hand and pointed the gun skywards with the other. He was laughing at Dusty, a mean laugh that didn't sound funny at all. Swags, eskies, slabs of beer, and camping gear were strewn around the clearing; there was mess everywhere.

Another tall, thin man was chopping up a dead kangaroo with an axe. The scene looked like something from hell, with blood and guts flying everywhere. Three tan-and-white hounds were salivating over the carcass, snarling and snapping at each other, leaping back in fright every time the axe came thudding down. Another man lay slumped against the side of the hut.

The cows started to spill into the clearing and Dusty backed up the Snow Pony to let them pass to the yards. They snorted and spooked at the mayhem in front of the hut, and trotted quickly through the open slip rails into the big yard—a paddock really, carpeted with clover and sheltered by snow gums.

As they ran past her dancing horse, Dusty noticed a

fourth person sitting in the front of the hunter's truck. The door was open and she sat sideways, her feet resting on the running board. A lanky deerhound sprawled over her lap and he looked as frightened as the girl.

She's been crying, thought Dusty, then realised the girl was staring back at her. She smiled at Dusty, a small frightened smile, and Dusty smiled back. It was Jade! Jade from school and the purple crystal tent. She looked so different in this strange environment that Dusty hardly recognised her.

The hounds began to bay, like prophets of doom. Dusty looked away from Jade and saw Jack and Stewie ride into the clearing. Digger and Spike were backed up under the horses, hackles up, as the hounds rushed and snarled at them. Spike, with his paw still strapped up, was vulnerable and knew it. He was yelping with fear. Jack lashed the hounds with his whip, cursing them, and finally the thin man looked up from the kangaroo carcass and called them to heel.

Stewie's face was ashen as he rode past Dusty. Captain looked like a warhorse, his mighty neck arched and his massive hooves thudding a staccato rhythm. Jack's face was grim. He didn't deign to look at the hunters, just nodded to Dusty and followed the last cows to the yards.

He had just swung the slip rails into place, Drover moving sideways with neat little steps, when the afternoon exploded in a barrage of shots. The two men had followed Jack to the yards and leant against the tangle of silver rails, shooting into the air and howling like idiots. The horses bucked and shied, spinning frantically. Captain backed into the truck, then shot forward with a leap that

117

flung Stewie out of the saddle. Dusty was fighting to control the Snow Pony, but as the world swirled crazily around her she saw her brother hit the ground with a sickening thud and lie as still and flat as a wet bag.

Captain thundered past the hut, stumbling on a swag and kicking the esky. The hounds milled around, baying, and Spike and Digger barked like lunatics. It was bedlam. The Snow Pony stopped spinning for a moment and Dusty threw her right leg over the pommel of the saddle and leapt off. She hit the ground running and raced to Stewie, but Jade was already there, cradling his head in her lap.

"He's all right, I think." She looked at Dusty desperately, then back at Stew. "You're all right, aren't you, mate?"

Stewie nodded groggily but his face was drained of colour. The girl's face was the same; white as a sheet.

Spike squirmed between them, looking for protection, and Dusty unbuckled his collar to release his paw. The shooting stopped. Dusty looked across to the yards, wondering what was going to happen next. The cattle had rushed into the far corner and milled there in a mad crush.

The hunters grinned stupidly as Jack rode up to them. He looked like Clint Eastwood, thought Dusty, in one of those cowboy movies where he tells the bad guys to get out and stay out. And that's what he did. Dusty couldn't hear what he said, his voice was so low, but he had a fierce authority about him that spoke louder than words. He stared down from his fidgeting horse and told them to go. The skinny one with the scary eyes started to say something, but the other one, Fatso, pulled him away from the fence and they turned back to their truck.

Dusty couldn't believe that her father could control the

situation like this, without raising his voice or even getting off his horse. Maybe it was because he *was* on horseback that they obeyed him, she thought. He looked right at home, as though this was his place and he was the boss.

He rode over to where Dusty and Jade knelt over Stewie, dismounted, and gave Dusty his reins. "How are you, mate?" he asked Stewie tenderly. The girl started to say something, but Jack cut her off. "Just go. Get that idiot," he motioned with a toss of his head at the young man slumped against the hut, "and get out of here. You and your mates have done enough damage." He gathered Stewie in his arms and carried him to the hut, pushing the door open with one leg and stepping through sideways.

Dusty caught the other horses and tied them up at the back of the hut. Jack had added a lean-to stable there when he was a young man, so the horses could have shelter when the weather got bad. They would be glad of it tonight. It was freezing already. When she walked around to the front of the hut the hunters had loaded their gear into the troop carrier, and everything looked less crazy. The two older men lifted the unconscious boy, one by the shoulders and the other by the feet, and half-carried, half-dragged him to the truck. Jade was sobbing wretchedly.

"What's wrong with him?" Dusty asked. "Is he hurt?"

"No." Her voice was bitter between the sobs. "He's just pissed. He's rotten drunk."

They flung him into the back of the truck carelessly—the way you'd throw a bag of chaff, thought Dusty—then called the hounds to jump in after him. The deerhound wouldn't jump in. He was a young dog and obviously

119

terrified of the others. He kept ducking under the truck until the skinny man caught him by his collar, hurled him up in one vicious swing, thudding against the inside of the truck, then slammed the door. The growls and terrified yelps told Dusty that he got the beating he was expecting from the hounds. Then there was silence.

She looked at Jade, standing alone between the truck and the hut, with her arms crossed over her chest. She wanted to talk to her, to ask her if she was all right, but just then Jack came out of the hut. He strode to the truck, and now that he was standing next to the hunters it seemed even more incredible that they had bowed to his orders. He was not a big man, neither tall nor heavy, and the fat hunter towered over him. The authority was still there, though. He was the boss.

"Get right off the plains tonight. It's going to snow, and snow plenty. You keep driving until you get to Banjo, you understand. And don't ever come back here."

Dusty thought Fatso was going to apologise for a moment, but the skinny one laughed scornfully and wrenched open the passenger-side door.

"Get in the truck!" he yelled at Jade, who moved across the clearing like a zombie and climbed in. He jumped in beside her and slammed the door. "Come on, Horse!" He held the horn down, filling the afternoon with its manic blare, until Fatso climbed behind the steering wheel, started the engine, and drove away.

The high-pitched whine of the motor, moving up and down through the gear changes as the truck wound up the ridge, took a long time to fade to nothing. Dusty looked at her father. It was hard to believe what had happened, now the intruders had gone. As they stood there, a last ray of sunlight shot through a gap in the clouds and lit up the far side of the clearing. The trees were suddenly bronze, glowing against the murky purple sky behind them.

"Look, Dad!" As suddenly as it had come, the light was gone and everything was grey again. Jack put his arm around her shoulders and, without any warning, Dusty burst into tears—not little weepy tears but great wrenching sobs that hurt her throat. Jack passed her a handkerchief and patted her back.

"It's all right, mate. They've gone now. We're all okay, and I'm proud of you."

No, I'm proud of you, thought Dusty, smiling at how much she had longed to hear him say those very words. She knew she wasn't just crying about what had just happened. She was crying for the last twelve months.

She went inside, still sniffing, and lit the fire while Jack fed and rugged the horses. Stewie was a silent lump on the bottom bunk, but as she positioned the billy over the flames a small voice came across the room.

"Is that you, Dad?"

Dusty went over and sat on the edge of the bunk. "No, it's me. How are you feeling?"

Stewie sat up and felt his head. "Good. I don't think I hit my head. I think I was just winded. What happened?"

"Dad told them to go." Dusty smiled at the memory. "And they did. He was fantastic, Stew. I couldn't hear what he said, but he looked like Clint Eastwood, staring down at them from Drover. They slunk off like dogs."

Jack came into the hut, pulling the door shut behind

121

him. "Digger and Spike are having a feast on that kanga-roo. Remind me to tie them up before we go to bed, Dusty. I don't trust Spike not to go stirring those cows up." He looked around the hut. "This looks pretty snug. How about you make a cup of tea, Dusty, while I rustle up some dinner? We've got snags and spuds and carrots and a tinned plum pudding for afters." He smiled across at Stewie. "You look good, son. It's a long way to fall, off a horse as big as Captain."

Dusty lit some of the candle stubs that sat in waxy saucers, but the main light came from the fire, flickering and golden. A gust of wind swirled around the hut, puffing smoke out of the fireplace and rattling the tin roof. It was going to be a dirty night. Dusty shivered.

"They won't come back, will they, Dad?"

Jack shook his head. "Not if they've got any sense. It's going to snow tonight for sure." He looked up from the fire and saw the worry on her face. "What's wrong?"

Dusty hesitated. "I feel sorry for that girl. They were awful men."

Jack snorted. "What are you worrying about her for? She'd be as tough as them. Did you see her clothes? No, she'd be able to handle herself, that one."

Dusty rolled a piece of warm wax between her fingers. "I don't know. She goes to my school. And I've seen her at the show, and at the market in Bankstown. She's okay. Her mum sells candles and stuff." She stared at the flaming wick. "You wouldn't like it if I was up here with two men like that." She said the last sentence very quietly and Jack either didn't hear it, or chose not to reply.

17

Jade's Run

The truck bounced along the track, climbing back up the spur to the high plains, its engine screaming through the gear changes like a devil. They were going way too fast, skidding around corners, thumping into potholes, rocking wildly on the rough track. Neville gripped the handle on the dashboard with one hand and Horse braced himself on the steering wheel, but everything else in the truck was getting bashed to bits. The noise inside the cabin was deafening. Jade was sitting on the toolbox, between the two front seats, and every bump was agony. The hounds yelped as they were flung about the back of the truck. Jade wondered about Travis and hoped his head was on something soft. Then she remembered how he had let her down by drinking himself into oblivion and decided that she didn't care.

Finally they stopped climbing and came out of the trees on to the high plains. The clouds were very low, hugging the tops of the trees. The landscape looked grey and lonely, just snow grass, rocks, and twisted snow gums.

"I need a beer." Horse braked suddenly and got out. Jade could hear him shifting gear in the back to reach the esky.

Neville nudged her with his knee. "Get some of this into ya." He was holding up the half-empty rum bottle.

Jade turned and looked at him for the first time since they left the hut. He had creepy eyes, like a lizard.

"No thanks."

He pressed his knee against her leg again and left it there, an insistent pressure. She twisted in her seat to see if Travis was awake, but he was still out to it, flopped like a dirty rag doll amongst the swags. Horse came back to the front of the car and put a six pack on the floor. He started to get in, then turned away. Jade thought he must have forgotten something, but he didn't walk to the back of the truck, just fiddled with the front of his clothes and urinated right there beside her. He was so close that Jade could smell the sour odour of his piss. Her stomach turned, not just from the stink, but from the knowledge that this wasn't right, that he had gone past the point of caring what she thought. She wasn't Jeannie's daughter any more, she was just a chick, like all the others they had sniggered about so foully for the last three days.

Her fears were well founded. "What more could you want, Nev?" Horse belched and sniggered as the truck bumped on again. "A couple a days of good hunting, plenty of grog, and a good lookin' sheila."

Neville swapped the rum bottle to his left hand and put his arm around Jade's shoulders. Jade looked straight ahead. Just ignore them, she told herself.

"Yeah, I reckon she'll do. I like 'em on the young side meself." Neville laughed slyly and suddenly reached down and grabbed Jade's breast. She turned to fight him and he pulled his hand away, then leant back against the door

124

and drained the bottle of rum in one long swallow, watching her all the while with his pale snake eyes. He didn't take his eyes off her as he tossed the empty bottle out the window and rubbed his hands together. "Gunna need two hands for this one I reckon." He smiled like a reptile and snapped his fists over Jade's wrists in a split second. "Come here, bitch."

He pulled her, kicking and screaming, on to his lap, transferred her skinny wrists into one vice-like hand, and shoved his free hand up under her shirt.

"Horse! Help me! Make him stop!" Jade was screaming and crying at the same time. The truck slowed down.

"Take it easy, mate," she heard Horse say, and felt him tugging at Neville's arm. "She's only a kid. What are you doing?"

Neville had jammed Jade's head under the glove box with his leg. She couldn't see anything apart from the tangled wiring under the dash, but she heard the unmistakable click of a safety catch being released.

"You just drive the truck, Fatty." Neville's voice was menacing. "Drive, and stay out of this or I'll blow your head off."

Jade's mind raced. She had to get away while he only had one hand to hold her. Once he'd put the gun back on the rack she'd have no hope.

"Let me up," she said. "I won't fight."

Neville shifted his leg so she could sit up. "I like a bit of spirit," he breathed in her face, so close she could see the spit in the corners of his mouth. He turned to put the gun back and as he did, Jade flung herself out the window, kicking desperately at the same time. She heard a

125

curse of pain as her foot connected with something. His grip on her wrists didn't shift until the momentum of the truck twisted his arm back and suddenly she was free. The ground knocked the wind out of her and the back wheel of the truck missed her head by inches.

She staggered to her feet as the tail lights glowed red, and stumbled off towards the trees, tripping over the snow grass, breathless and shaking with fear. A shot rang out and she started to run. Suddenly, insanely, she remembered a movie she'd seen once, a comedy, where people being shot at were running across an airstrip, yelling, "Serpentine! Serpentine!" The trees were getting closer and she glanced back over her shoulder. The truck was racing after her like a mad thing, almost airborne as it hit logs and ditches. Horse had turned on the headlights and the artificial light danced against the trees in front of her like a crazy slide show.

Jade ran like a greyhound, past the snow gums on the edge of the plain, jumping logs and rocks, running deeper and deeper into the darkness of the bush until she felt sure she was hidden. She dropped into a hollow behind an old overturned tree and lay low, her breath coming back in long noisy gasps. After a little while she stood up and carefully peered over the log, terrified that she would see Neville with his gun, stalking her through the bush. He hadn't followed her. Through the trees she could see him in the truck, gun out the window, as Horse drove to and fro along the tree line, trying to spot her. He started to call out. "Jade! Come out! I won't hurt you!" Jade could hear him laughing. "Come here, Jade! Come here, pussy cat! Here pussy, pussy, pussy. Ha ha ha." Jade didn't move. Suddenly a shot ripped into the trees and he started to shout again. "Stay here then, you stupid cow!" He sounded as if he was frothing at the mouth. "Stay here and starve!"

The truck stopped and she could hear him guffawing with Horse, and muttering. Then came a wild yelping as Stringer was flung out the window. "Starve with this shit of a dog that you like so much!"

Stringer ran for the trees, and Jade's heart stopped, waiting for Neville to gun him down, but the shot never came. The truck spun around, revving, and lurched away across the plain, its headlights zigzagging up and down as the vehicle bounced over the snow grass.

Stringer came straight to Jade, crept up to her, and his sad hairy face was so comical she had to smile. She put her arms around him and winced as she felt the pain in her wrists for the first time. The noise of the truck faded to nothing and there was no colour left in the day. Night was falling and she had never felt so cold or so alone. Her arms and legs began to shake violently, in uncontrollable spasms. Her teeth chattered and she cried out, terrified that her body was behaving this way. After a little while the shakes lessened. She took some deep breaths and remembered Jeannie reacting the same way last year, after the milk truck had crashed into their car. "It was the shock," she explained later; it was just her body reacting to the shock. She wished her mum was with her and started to cry, but then thought about what Jeannie would do, and she forced herself to stand up.

"Come on, dog," she said to Stringer. "It's a long way back to the hut, but that's where we've got to go. That dad looked pretty unfriendly, but I think he's okay. And I know the girl from school."

She zipped her jacket up and wished Jeannie had bought her a longer, warmer, more sensible one, instead of a groovy metallic blue crop-top with fake fur around the hood and the cuffs. She pulled the hood over her head, tied the drawstring tight under her chin and felt warmer immediately. When she was little and hated wearing hats, Jeannie was always telling her how important it was to keep her head warm. She could hear her now, using her grannie's voice, "You lose ninety per cent of your body heat through your head, young lady, so get that hat on before I give you Larry Dooley."

Thinking of her mother's funny ways made her feel less alone. She started to walk back to the track, staying among the trees in case the truck returned. The snow gums huddled together like twisted human figures. They were gnarled and striped, with crinkles in their silver bark like the creases in her elbows. Her hands were hurting with cold, so she pulled the sleeves of her jumper through her jacket cuffs and wrapped them around her fingers like mittens. Stringer bounded along beside her with his funny loping stride, smiling as though this was the best adventure he could have hoped for. When they reached the track, Jade started to run. She needed to warm up, and she needed to get as far as she could before it got completely dark. It was very dim already. She settled into a steady jog.

As she ran, she tried to work out how far it was back to the hut. She had left her watch at home, so her estimates were all guesses, but she thought it had taken about half an hour to get from the hut up to the plains. Even though it had felt as though the truck were flying, they had probably been doing only about thirty kilometres an hour. Jade remembered looking down at the speedo during a really fast bit, and the needle was wavering around forty. That made it about fifteen kilometres away. "Lucky I'm good at maths, hey, dog," she called to Stringer.

She had run that far before, with Dad, when she went to stay with him in the last holidays, and it had taken them just under one and a half hours. "That was uphill a long way, though, dog." Stringer turned back to her with his head on one side and a puzzled expression on his face. "This is downhill all the way. Easy peasy for runners like us."

She ran on, watching the ground carefully as the light dimmed. She couldn't afford to fall or sprain her ankle. She was depending on her legs to save her life. She laughed aloud at that thought—it was so dramatic, but it was true. She strode out on the flat stretches, jumping puddles and skirting muddy bits, and powered up the inclines, but on the steep descents she ran with little bitty steps—"old geezer steps" Dad used to call them—to make sure she didn't slip.

It was lucky after all that she'd worn her runners. Horse had told her off on the first day for her light footwear. "You need boots like these," he'd pointed to his own big clodhoppers. "This is tough country we're going to." Jade snorted to herself, remembering the conversation. Horse could have worn ballet slippers on the trip because he'd never been more than about ten steps away from the truck.

"He's a big bag of wind," she said to Stringer, loping beside her. He grinned his whiskery grin, as if to say, "Yes, Jade, of course, whatever you say. You're wonderful, Jade, you're the very best."

She stopped running after a little while, because the bare strip between her top and her jeans was hurting with the cold. She wished she'd listened to her nanna, who was always telling her to tuck her shirt in. "You'll get a chill in your kidneys, young lady." Nan was so keen on singlets and spencers that she wore them *under* her bra, and she thought anyone with a bare midriff was just asking for trouble. Jade pulled her top down and her jeans up, but they came apart as soon as she moved. She patted her hands over her jacket. If she had some safety pins she could pin them together. "Ah ha!" She felt her woollen scarf. She didn't need that around her neck, now that her jacket was done up. She wound the scarf carefully around her waist, zipping her jeans over it and pulling her jacket down. Her hands were stinging with the cold, so she pulled her jumper cuffs over them and set off again.

The bush around her was silent. Jade hadn't seen a bird or animal since she started running. Once, she heard footsteps behind her and thought she was being chased, and then the bush felt dark and dangerous. She panicked for a moment, and ran like the wind, but when the footsteps behind her got faster, too, she realised it was the sound of her own steps.

It was very dark now and she could only see where she was going by following the sky above the track, where it glowed slightly paler than the trees. The moon was out there somewhere, behind the banks of cloud. Her eyes felt as big as golf balls, straining to see in the gloom. Something landed on her face, something very cold, then another and another. Suddenly it was snowing, thick heavy snow, falling out of the sky in swirling eddies. It was as though someone were shaking a giant sieve of icing sugar on the land. Jade smiled to think of God jiggling Nan's sifter to and fro over the high plains. She looked down at Stringer to tell him her funny thought and realised that the snow had in fact been heaven-sent. She could see him clearly against the snow, his dark grey coat standing out like . . .

"Like dog's balls!" Jade said to him. "You're sticking out like dog's balls, Stringer." Now she had something to follow. "Go on, boy!" She urged him ahead with a wave of her arm. "Take me to the hut!"

He ran ahead and Jade could see him easily, her hairy guide, loping through the snow like a shadow.

18
Out of the Night

Dusty wriggled her toes inside their warm woollen socks and leant back in her favourite chair. Years ago, an anonymous visitor had carved it with a chainsaw from a single snow gum stump, tilting the seat slightly backwards and leaving a long leaning section of trunk intact for the back. Like the bunks and table, years of use had given the wood a sleek patina. It felt wonderful to be warm and dry.

A line of boots sat in front of the fire—Dad's, Stewie's, and hers—drying out for tomorrow. Stewie was asleep with firelight flickering over his face. Dusty could hear the horses stamping in their stalls on the other side of the wall. She loved living like this, everyone in together.

"Come and see this, Dusty." Jack was standing in front of the window, peering through the smoky panes of glass. "It's been snowing and we didn't even know. Look. The wind's died right away and the snow is just falling out of the sky."

They huddled together at the tiny view for a moment, then went outside and stood shivering under the verandah. Swirls of fat white flakes floated silently down around them, and the ground in front of the hut had transformed into a thick white carpet.

Dusty jumped up and down with excitement. It was as though magic had happened. "Oh, Dad, isn't it beautiful! Snow, lovely snow."

Jack pulled a face. "You mightn't think it's so lovely tomorrow. If it keeps it up at this rate, we'll be snowed in by morning." He opened the door to the hut and the light from within turned the flakes into dancing pieces of gold. "Come inside. It's too cold for anyone out here."

Dusty pulled her beanie low over her ears and wriggled down into her sleeping-bag, snug as a bug in a rug. She was very tired, and sleep was creeping up on her like a warm summer tide, when Digger barked so loudly that she snapped wide awake. It was a terrified bark, a there's-something-out-there bark: "Woo woo woo." Spike joined in, yapping hysterically.

Jack jumped down from the top bunk.

"What is it, Dad? Have they come back?" Dusty had goose bumps on her arms.

"I don't know. There's something there, though."

The dogs kept barking, their chains rattling the sides of the kennels as they paced to and fro.

"I wish we'd brought the gun." Dusty's voice sounded as wobbly as she felt.

"Stay there. Stay in bed." Jack patted her lightly on the shoulder, peered out the window, and walked towards the door.

Dusty looked across at Stewie, who was sleeping through the din. "Don't go out there, Dad," she hissed at

133

him, but he picked up the poker from the fireplace and stepped outside.

Dusty wanted to rush to the window, but she felt paralysed with fear. The barking changed pitch abruptly—the fear was gone—and Dusty thought at first that the dogs had taken heart because Jack was outside. But then she realised that they could see what was out there and it didn't frighten them. Spike whined excitedly and Digger growled softly.

"Bloody hell!" Jack's voice, muffled through the wall, was disbelieving. "Here, boy! Here, pup."

Dusty jumped out of bed. The door swung open before she reached it.

"Come and look at this, Dusty."

The dog had snow caught in his bushy eyebrows and he was so tall that Dusty thought for a moment he was a deer.

"It's the girl's dog, the one she was holding." Her mind raced. "D'you think he fell off the truck? Maybe he ran away."

The dog spread his legs and shook the snow off his back, then went to run back into the night. Dusty grabbed his collar, and he struggled and whined, staring towards the track. She followed his eyes, and through the falling snow saw a figure staggering across the clearing. It was the girl. It was Jade. Before they could step out to meet her she was under the verandah, hunched over, hands on her knees, gasping air into her lungs in huge sucking breaths.

"Come inside, quick." Jack touched her elbow. "You'll freeze in no time out here."

Dusty stepped back to let Jade past. Her face was bright red, and her shiny jacket with its pointy hood made her look like a spacewoman.

Jack put his leg in front of the dog to stop him coming into the hut, but when he saw the girl's face drop he changed his mind. The dog slipped through the doorway like a shadow and sat neatly on one side of the fire as if to say, "I'll be no trouble, no trouble at all."

Dusty pulled a blanket off the top bunk and wrapped it around Jade's shoulders.

"Thanks." Her breathing was less ragged. "I hope you don't mind me coming back here," she held her hands out to the fire, "but they . . . they attacked me. Travis was flaked out, and I think Neville was gunna kill me. I jumped out the truck window, up on that big plain." Her voice broke into sobs as she spoke, and Dusty could only just understand what she was saying.

Jack was kneeling at the hearth, putting another log on the fire. "Don't tell me they're coming back here." His voice was impatient, and Dusty patted Jade's shoulder, to make up for her father's bad manners.

"No. They kept going. They were heading for the road. The sign said it was ten kilometres."

Jack spun around. "You were up *there*? Up at the top plain? But that's a good sixteen ks. You'd have never made it by now."

"I ran."

Dusty and Jack looked at her in disbelief.

"I know how to run. My dad taught me."

Jack smiled at her for the first time. "And he taught you well. That's a mighty long way on a good day, but to do

135

it at night in a blizzard is something else." He put his hand out. "What's your name, young lady?"

"It's Jade, Dad. I told you, I know her from school." Dusty looked sideways at Jade and tried a joke. "We're the lonely girls."

Jack looked at her strangely. He didn't know what a rotten time she had at school.

"It doesn't matter, Dad."

Jade smiled at her though; she knew what the lonely club was.

Stewie was still sound asleep in his bunk; he hadn't heard a thing. Jack told the girls about the time when he and Rita had taken a noisy party of friends to see their sleeping baby son, and even that ruckus hadn't woken him up. Jade was beginning to shiver in her wet clothes, so Jack found an assortment of spare clothes for her.

"I'll go to bed so you can get changed. Make sure you take all your stuff off, because even the inside layers will be wet. And you should probably share Dusty's bunk, Jade, so you get a bit of her body heat. You could feel really cold after that big effort." He kissed Dusty and patted Jade on the back. "Goodnight, girls."

Jade and Dusty sat in front of the fire together, sipping the hot chocolates Jack had made before he got back into bed. Jade felt as dry as a chip in her borrowed clothes.

"Do you mind sharing a bed?" Dusty did feel a bit strange about it, but she couldn't say so.

"No, it'll be fine." Jade coughed nervously. "Um, actually I do feel a bit weird about it because I stink."

Dusty started to say she didn't mind, but Jade cut her off.

"*I* do. I haven't had a wash since Sunday night and I think it's Wednesday now. That's three days." She held a hank of hair under her nose and sniffed. "My hair stinks of smoke, too, from the campfire and their cigarettes."

"I've got just the thing for you." Dusty stood on her stool, reached up to the rafters, and juggled down a big tin tub. "Mum used to bathe us in this when we were little." She rapped her knuckles against the tin—bong, bong. "She and I still use it when we're feeling really grotty."

Jade hesitated and glanced at the bunks. "What if your dad gets up, or your brother?"

Dusty pulled the faded tartan blanket off Jade's shoulders and pegged it to the clothesline hanging across the room. "For you, Mees Jade, we 'ave the special privacy curtain." She laughed. "And I'll look the other way. Come on, there's two billies here with hot water in them."

Jade squeezed warm water from the towelling washcloth so that it ran over her face and down her chest. It felt good to be clean, and the heat from the fire warmed her front. She picked up the soap to lather her arms and it shot out of her hand like a frog. Dusty handed it back and couldn't help noticing the bruises on Jade's arms and three ugly welts running diagonally across her ribs.

Jade saw her looking. "I fell over a fair bit on the way here. That's how I got these." She held up her elbows. "But these," she touched her wrists and peered at her ribs, "these are from Neville." She pressed the washcloth against her face as she remembered the fight. "But I got him. I reckon I kicked him in the nose, didn't I, dog?"

Stringer lay with his head on his paws. He opened one eye and nodded his head slightly. The girls laughed out loud at him and then sat together in silence, each lost in their thoughts.

Dusty was thinking how different Jade was from her. She couldn't imagine herself fighting a grown man, or running sixteen kilometres. She remembered that day at the Bankstown Show, when she had seen Jade selling her mother's candles and envied her wild clothes and easy manner. She blushed as she remember her arrogant assumption that Jade would be soft and impractical, not a tough farm girl like her.

"You're a hero, Jade. I can't imagine doing what you've just done."

Jade laughed. "I can't imagine it either. I've always been a little nobody. Sometimes I feel like a shadow at home, there's always so much going on. Mum's always got to do just one more thing before she can get to me, always has one more phone call to make. Trav hardly talks to me. And Dad, well Dad's so far away that sometimes I forget what he looks like."

Jade thought how angry her mother was going to be when she found out what had happened. It would be the end of Horse, and she would have the police after Neville. She'd want to kill Travis. The image of her brother's body in the back of the truck flashed into her mind. "I hope he's all right."

"Who?"

"Travis. My brother. He was the drunk one. The unconscious drunk one. God, I hate what grog does to people."

Dusty nodded, "Me, too."

Jade looked up and Dusty saw her disbelief. "I know. I know what grog does to people," she said softly, aware of her father in his bunk on the other side of the blanket. "We've had a bad time because of it."

Jade raised her eyebrows in surprise. It was hard to believe this perfect family was flawed. "Hey, pass me the towel, will you?"

Dusty pressed it to her cheek before handing it to Jade. It was warm from hanging beside the fire.

"Where are your mum and dad?" Dusty asked, and Jade told her their complicated family situation.

"Trav rang Mum from Banjo on Monday afternoon and we left the phone off the hook so she'd think it was engaged if she rang. She thinks I've been at school all week."

Dusty tried to imagine doing something so wilful, but she couldn't. Everything she did involved her parents. "Won't she worry when she can't get through on the phone?"

Jade shook her head. "She never worries. She always thinks things are going to be all right. I worry more than her." She rubbed her head with the towel. "I'm really worried about Travis. Horse is just plain stupid, but that Neville is a mean bastard." She peered at Dusty's watch. "They should be off the high plains by now, back in civilisation. When Trav gets home and wakes up he's going to have a mighty hangover, but then he's going to want to know where I am, and he's going to ring Mum and she'll ring the police . . . oh boy, what a mess."

∾

Jade lay on her side, eyes closed, and waited for sleep to come. She could feel Dusty's body behind her, settled in the same shape. "Pretend we're riding a bike," she'd said.

"That's what Mum says when we share a bed." Jade wondered what Jeannie was doing tonight in the city, so far from the high plains, but she was too tired to concentrate. Her thoughts flicked from one thing to another, disturbing flashes from the long day. Just before she fell asleep she remembered Jack's smile when she said, "My dad taught me to run." It was like saying, "I'm special. Someone cares for me. I can do something really well." It made her feel good.

19
Snowed In

Jade felt sore all over when she woke up. The dad, Jack, and the little brother were moving around the hut, speaking in murmurs, putting more wood on the fire, rustling through plastic bags, and getting food from the cupboard. She hoped they'd be going home today. She just wanted to be in her own house, with Jeannie, and maybe ring up Dad, not stuck with this family she didn't know. She could imagine how snobby the dad would be to Jeannie. As she listened to their movements, Jade realised there were no noises coming from outside the hut. The outside world was silent. Stringer whined and she heard the door groan open.

"Holy hell! Look at this, Stew." The door swung shut and their voices were muffled, but she could still hear the excitement. There must be a lot of snow out there, she thought.

"Hey, horses!" His voice was deep and soft, coming from around the back of the hut. The horses whinnied. She listened to him tipping feed into buckets and filling their water, talking to them all the time. The horses nickered softly as they waited to be fed, and Jade realised that they all had different whinnies. One had a high "hehehehe," another sounded as if it just couldn't wait, "hoo hoo hoo," and the third horse was quite musical, "whoo hoo hmm hmm." She'd always thought horses just went "neigh."

The floorboard beside her bunk creaked and she opened her eyes. The little brother was standing, staring at her. His ginger hair stuck out in all directions and his ears poked out, too. He was very slight and bursting with excitement.

"I let your dog outside." He peered over her to see if Dusty was awake. "He wanted to go out so I let him. You should see him playing in the snow. He's crazy!"

Jack carried a steaming mug from the table and handed it to Jade. "White with one?"

She nodded and propped herself on one elbow. "Ow. Thank you."

"Jade, this is Stewie. He's been busting for you to wake up. He thought Dusty had multiplied when he saw you there." Stewie pulled a face. "But don't hurry to get up. It's freezing and we won't be going anywhere today. There's a metre of snow out there."

The blankets behind Jade heaved and Dusty sat up, rubbing her eyes. "Are we snowed in?" She looked at the windows, but they were iced over. "Has winter come early, like in that old newspaper story? What does it mean, Dad? Are we stuck here? Can we get the cows out?"

Stewie swung on the end of the bunk, his eyes wide. "We've got to stay here *aaaall* winter. We'll have to eat the cows."

Jack smiled. "We won't be here all winter. Jokes aside, if it came to that they'd send a helicopter in for us." He walked over to the door and opened it slightly. "It's eased off a bit, but it's still snowing. I reckon it'll rain later and wash the snow away, or at least pack it down, so we can get out tomorrow. The weather map on Monday showed a high pressure system coming over the Bight, and that normally means higher temperatures, but I think this is coming up from the south east. The weather can do anything up here. Cuppa, Dusty?"

He squatted in front of the fire to pour her tea.

"What if it doesn't rain? What if it keeps snowing?" Dusty's mind was full of questions. What about the cows? They'd been out in the snow all night. What about Mum? She'd expect them to be at The Plains tonight. If a helicopter had to come in to rescue them, what would happen to the horses? She blurted them out in one long sentence and Jack outlined their situation as she sipped her tea.

What they had to realise, he explained, was that the snow would be much deeper up on the top plains, at the house; it would be over their heads. It was colder there, so more snow would have fallen. The further you got down the mountains the less snow there was. If it kept snowing, they might have to go down, to try to ride out on the old bridle track, but it was very overgrown and there were dangerous places where the track had fallen into the river.

Secondly, it was unlikely that this was the beginning of winter. There would almost certainly be a break in the weather when they could get the stock out, even if they had to feed them in the meantime. He and Rita had brought bags of chaff and oats to the hut when they had

143

driven out in February, so there was feed for the horses, but there was nothing for the cows. They could survive a few days without food, as long as they had water.

"Are they covered with snow?" Jade asked, and Stewie laughed.

"They've got white backs, but they look quite happy."

Jack poured oatmeal into the billy to make porridge. "They're all camped together, up near the spring. I had to climb up on the side of the hut to see them because the snow is right up to the top rail of the yards. They've tramped the snow down as it's fallen around them, and their body heat has melted some, too, so it's as though they're standing in a hole."

Stewie laughed again. "When Jade asked if they were covered with snow, I imagined them in a big snowy cave."

Jack stirred the porridge. "Well, that's not as silly as it sounds. I haven't heard of it happening with cattle, but old Mr. MacNamara told me once that he found sheep like that. His family had ewes that got caught in early snow on the plains, and when they rode out to look for them there was not a sheep to be seen. They thought they'd all perished. They were about to go home when someone noticed steam rising from a hole in the snow, then another, and another. When they dug down they found the sheep in caverns under the snow. They had to dig them out, and then push a path through the snow with their horses, but they saved most of them."

∾

The verandah had been transformed into a room—a room with walls of icy blue snow. Dusty couldn't believe her eyes when she stepped outside. The snow had fallen so

144

quietly that it hadn't drifted under the verandah at all, just settled down in a straight bank. There was a gap of about a metre between the top of the snow and the verandah, and the world looked very beautiful through it—white and silent with fat individual snowflakes floating down. At the western end of the hut the snowy walls were smashed and flattened where Stewie had been playing with the dogs.

"Come and see her mad dog, Dusty. He and Spike are having the best time." Stewie grabbed her hand and they ran out the opening he had made. The snow flew around them, as light and dry as goose down. Jade came outside, too, and Stringer bounded up to her with a great kangaroo leap that sent her flying backwards in the snow. He licked her face and when she screamed, raced off like a lunatic and buried his head in the snow. Then he jumped up, grinning and covered with white, and raced in the other direction. Digger watched from the verandah. He was too old for games. But Spike tore after the hound, trying to keep up with him.

Grey clouds filled the sky, so not a glimmer of sun got through. Each falling snowflake was stark white against the dull landscape. Jade had never seen snow like it.

"When we went to the snow it was really wet and horrible. Nothing like this." She shook her head and the snow flew off her hair like powder.

"There's lots of different types of snow." Dusty was trying to make a snowball but the snow wouldn't stick together. "They say the Inuit, the people from the north pole, have about a hundred different words for snow. I guess because they live in it all the time, it's not just

145

snow, it's wet heavy snow or wet light snow, or snow that sticks to your feet, always some sort of snow."

"Don't get your clothes wet, kids." Jack was wading along the side of the hut, white fluff billowing around him. "We haven't got many spares." He stood with them, laughing at Stringer bounding after sticks and diving into the snow. "He's a character all right. We'll have to tie him up this afternoon, though, because we've got a job to do in the yards. I've just been up to check the cows and there's a calf there with a broken leg. She must have been trampled when those idiots were shooting yesterday."

Jade blushed and Jack noticed. "It's not your fault, Jade," he said kindly.

Dusty thought what a difference it made to meet some-one, and talk to them, rather than deciding who they were by the way they looked. She was glad Jade couldn't hear the harsh words Jack had had for her yesterday.

"Anyway," Jack went on. "I'm going to try and put a splint on her leg. And wouldn't you know, it's that stupid old roan cow's calf. You know the one, Dusty, with the hook horns?"

"She's as mad as a snake."

"Yep, we'll have to be careful. That's why I said we'll have to tie up the dogs. Don't want them stirring things up."

∾

Jade stood on an up-ended log, combing the knots out of Captain's mane. She had never been close to such a big horse and felt frightened when she first stepped into the stable. He'd looked so fierce and powerful when she'd seen him yesterday. Dusty reassured her by swinging on to his back from the fence and sprawling there like a model in a car advertisement. "Come ride with me," she purred, playing the role. "Feel the horse power under you." She realised suddenly that she was being like Sally, being the funny one, and it felt good. She slithered off the big horse and adjusted his woollen rug. "I think navy blue is your colour, Captain." She ducked underneath him to check the other side. "Don't you think he looks handsome, Jade?"

Jade thought he was the most beautiful horse she had ever seen. The only other horses she had been this close to were at the Happy Valley Riding School, near Bankstown, and they were scrawny little ponies. This horse was so big she couldn't see over his back, and he was as solid as a house. If he put his head up in here it would touch the roof. Dusty introduced her to Drover and the Snow Pony. They were beautiful horses, too, but Captain was the one she liked best. Drover was quiet and aloof. He accepted attention but it was as though he was saying, "That's enough fussing now, I'm a working horse, not a pet."

"Don't they kick each other?" Jade asked. "I thought they'd all be in separate stalls."

"No, they get on okay. The Snow Pony and Captain are in love, and Drover keeps to himself." Dusty pushed Captain aside with her shoulder and Jade was amazed how happily the big horse obeyed her. She moved amongst the horses as easily as Jade would walk down a supermarket aisle. "It's important to let them huddle together, so they keep each other warm."

Dusty told Jade the story of the Snow Pony as they petted her. Jade could see that the beautiful mare adored

147

her, breathing against Dusty's neck and nuzzling her hands.

"Be careful of her though, Jade. She's a pain with people she doesn't know. I guess it's all those years of living in the bush, when she had to rely on her wits to survive. Mum says she has a very well developed flight instinct."

Jade reached up to pat Snow's forehead and the mare snorted and threw her head up.

"See what I mean? She's just highly strung."

While Jade worked on Captain's mane, Dusty filled the water drum and shovelled the horse manure from the dirt floor out into the snow. At the far end of the lean-to was a small room, where the feed drums and spare gear was stored, but the other sides of the verandah weren't closed in. Crooked rails, wired to the verandah posts, formed a fence to keep the horses in, and a wall of snow had formed behind them. Hollows in the snow marked where the horses' warm breath had melted the snow as they looked out the gap between the snow and the roof.

Dusty put the shovel away and came back with Captain's bridle. "Do you want to have a ride on him? Let's surprise Dad and Stewie."

Jade looked doubtful, but Dusty grinned at her as she bridled Captain, guiding the bit gently between his teeth and pulling the headpiece over his ears in one smooth action.

"You'll probably double-dink with Stewie tomorrow, anyway, so you might as well have a practice now. You'll be okay, I promise. I'll go in front and you can hang on to me." She led the horse out of the stable and replaced the slip rails, then backed him around so that he stood beside the fence.

Dusty climbed up the fence and scrambled on to him. Jade followed quickly, before she had time to chicken out. She put her arms around Dusty's waist and held on tight as Captain moved away from the hut. There were no bones poking into her like the other time she had ridden bareback. Riding this horse was like sitting in an armchair, he was so round and comfortable, and his walk was slow and even. Jade relaxed slightly and drew her head away from Dusty's back so she could see. The snow was still falling lightly, with big flakes that drifted around them, and the powder flew up as Captain moved through it. They could have been floating through the snow.

Dusty turned her head. "Are you right for a canter?"

Jade didn't have a chance to say no. She held on to Dusty as Captain broke into a canter, expecting to bounce straight off, but it was like sitting on a rocking horse.

"Hey, Dad! Stewie! Come and see the snow circus!"

They cantered past the hut, sending up showers of snow. "We are the alpine trick riders!" Dusty guided the big horse with her legs, making a circle in front of the hut, and held her arms up in a V. Stringer loped beside them, grinning over his shoulder. Jack and Stewie watched from the verandah, laughing, and Dusty whooped. "Isn't this good, Jade? Isn't he the best?"

Jade loosened her grip on Dusty's waist and raised one hand in the air, waving. Her seat didn't shift. Riding had never been so easy.

"Yes!" she shouted. "He's the best!"

149

20
The Roan Cow

Jade and Stewie watched from outside the yards as Jack explained to Dusty how they were going to catch the calf. They would never run it down, even though it had a broken leg, so Jack had rigged up a makeshift trap by wiring an old mesh gate to the fence and propping it open at a slight angle. He and Dusty were going to walk quietly through the mob, push a group of cows and calves along the fence, and try to jam the injured calf behind the gate. Jade and Stewie were to stand as still as statues until the calf walked in, and then they had two jobs: to pull the gate towards them to hold the calf tight, then shove a rail behind her so she couldn't back out.

"The mother is as crazy as a loon," Jack told Jade, "but she won't get over this fence. You'll be safe here." He handed Dusty a stick. "Are we all ready? Remember, you two, keep still. Don't move a muscle. And you, Stewie, make sure you pay attention. Don't muck up this time."

Stewie made a face and Dusty wished her dad would give him a break.

It was sickening to see the calf hobbling on three legs, its broken shin flapping uselessly.

150

"You be ready to get over the fence if that cow even looks at you, Dusty." Jack guided her through the yard as cows and calves scrambled out of their way, snow slipping off their backs. "Your mother would have my guts for garters if she knew you were in here, but it's a two-person job. I'll push the cattle towards the fence and you be ready to rush the calf behind the gate."

Jack let most of the mob past him until there were only about six cows left, with their calves. "Push them along now, Dusty," he called to her quietly.

Dusty walked towards the cows, arms out. "Come on, girls, ho, ho."

The roan cow was in the middle of the mob, head up, and her calf was just where they wanted it, at the back, near the fence.

"Looking good, Dad," Dusty murmured.

The cow at the front of the group started to walk behind the gate, then stopped when her shoulders jammed. Jade and Stewie held their breath, then she backed out and moved along, with the others following. Dusty crept closer to the calf, ready to block her if she shied away, but she walked behind the gate without hesitation, and Jade and Stewie pulled it tight. She bawled in fright as Dusty scrambled over the fence and helped shove the rail behind her and tie the gate.

"What a team!" Jack was out of the yard, too. "You've got her as tight as a pressed flower." He held the splint he had improvised out of wire and wood beside the calf's broken leg. "Yep, I think it's going to work. The knee will stop it riding up and the fetlock will stop it falling down."

The roan cow bellowed on the other side of the fence.

Jack reached through the rails and fitted the two pieces of wood around the calf's foreleg. She bleated in pain as he manipulated the fracture, and her mother roared like an angry dinosaur.

"Pliers please, Stewie." He held his arm behind him and Stewie placed the pliers in his hand like a nurse in an operating theatre. "There you go," Jack grunted as he twisted the wire together, holding the broken leg firmly between two pieces of wood. "That should make life easier for her." He stood up and rubbed his hands together. "Let her out and we'll go inside and warm up and pray for rain."

Dusty removed the rail from behind the calf, and Stewie untied the gate and pushed it away from the fence. The calf turned and went to join its bellowing mother. Its first steps were steady, and Dusty smiled to think they had made such a difference, but suddenly the calf fell over and lay writhing on the trampled snow. Every time she tried to get up the splinted leg collapsed underneath her, and Dusty's first traitorous thought was that Jack must have done something terribly wrong to her leg, something that made it worse instead of better.

"It's caught on the gate!" Stewie yelled to Jack above the bawling and bellowing. "The wire on the splint is hooked on the gate!"

Jack swore violently. "Give us the pliers again. I'll bend those ends down before I let her go this time." He went to climb over the fence and Jade looked at Dusty, eyes wide.

"He's not getting in the yard with that cow, is he?"

"He has to." Dusty picked up the branch she had carried in the yard and climbed on to the fence. "He can't leave the calf stuck there. He'll keep the calf between him and the cow, and the gate will give him some protection."

Stewie was very pale, his face yellow against the snow. "Be careful, Dad."

Jack pulled the gate closer to the fence and inched up to the struggling calf. The cow rushed up, snorting, and glared at him over her baby, saliva hanging from her mouth in long dribbles. Jack kept his eyes on her, reached down the splint and unhooked the wire, then briefly looked down as he crimped the wire flat. He pushed the calf to her feet and she ran to her mother, who nuzzled her then turned back to the mob. But suddenly Spike was in the yard, silently heeling the calf. When it bawled, the mother bellowed at Spike, and raced at him, horns lowered and dangerous, and the dog ran straight to Jack. Jack was lifting the gate to lean it flush against the fence, so the cow's charge took him by surprise. As he turned towards the noise, her head caught him across the ribs with a sickening crack and sent him thudding to the ground.

"Dad!" Dusty leapt into the yard and swung her stick at the cow. "Get back, you old bitch." The cow rushed at her, eyes crazy, and Dusty dived through the fence.

Spike ran behind the cow, yapping, and Dusty could see that her father was in a bad way. He was trying to crawl through the fence, but the mesh of the old gate was in the way. He was as helpless as a baby. When the cow charged back, pawing and trying to hook him with her ferocious horns, all he could do was roll into a ball.

Stewie leant over the fence, screaming, whipping

153

desperately at her face with the rope. Dusty jumped into the yard again, screaming too, and swung her stick at the cow, but had to turn and race for her life. Spike was still heeling the cow and when she turned on him this time, Jade jumped down from the fence and ran into the yard.

"Get him out!" She was waving her shiny blue jacket. "Pull him under the fence."

The cow turned, and it was terrifying to see her furious anger focused on Jade's slight figure.

"She'll kill you!" Dusty screamed, but Jade wasn't listening. She darted in front of the cow like a gnat, flicking the blue jacket, drawing her away from Jack.

"Dusty!" Stewie slapped her. "Help me with Dad!"

Jack moaned as they grabbed his arms. Dusty could hardly breathe for the racking sobs that choked up her throat. They slid him easily across the packed snow and shoved him under the bottom rail, then climbed through themselves and pulled him over the snow until he was completely clear.

"Stay with him, Stew." Dusty flew over the fence and saw Jade and Spike playing a mad game of cat and mouse with the cow. As soon as she turned on one, the other would taunt her. Dusty knew the cow would finally win that game. She ran towards them, waving her arms. "Get out, Jade! Get out when she chases me!" She scrambled to the top of the fence as the cow roared towards her, and when she looked across, Jade was safe as well. Spike shot under the fence. "Get back to the hut, you mongrel," screamed Dusty.

Stewie knelt in the snow, cradling his father's head between his knees. His tears splashed on to Jack's face, and Dusty felt sick when she saw how battered it was. Blood oozed out of a gash on his temple, and one eye was already closed with swelling.

"Is he conscious?" Stewie nodded. "Can you hear me, Dad?" Dusty packed some snow into her glove and held it against his temple. Jack moaned and opened his good eye.

"I'm all right." His voice was a whisper. "I'm hurt, but I'm not going to die. I think my ribs are busted."

Jade dropped beside him on the snow, panting desperately. "Is he okay?"

Dusty tried to push down the panic that bubbled up in her chest. She felt as if she might vomit, but someone needed to do something and it had to be her. She tried to think clearly, logically.

"We need to get you off the snow, Dad." She looked at the hut, about fifty metres away. "Do you think you can walk?"

Jack grimaced and closed his eye. "Should be able to." His voice was still just a whisper. He was fighting for breath. "Just give me a minute."

Dusty could feel the cold creeping into her bones as the snow fell around them. "No, Dad, you've got to get up now. You'll get hypothermia if you stay here. We've got to get you inside."

She knelt and slid her hand underneath his shoulder. Jade reached under, too, until their hands overlapped. "We'll sit you up first. Are you ready?" She realised she was talking like a nurse. "One, two, three . . ."

"Aaaarrghh!" Jack moaned, an animal cry, and the girls gently laid him flat again. His face was deathly pale.

"Don't," Stewie begged her. "Don't hurt him worse. You might make him a paraplegic."

"What about a mattress?" Jade's brain was going at a hundred miles an hour, too. "What if we put him on a mattress and drag him to the hut?"

"It'd be pretty bumpy." Dusty looked at Stewie. "I don't think he's got a broken back, Stewie. I'm sure it's his ribs. You could hear them snap when the cow hit him." Jade nodded. "It's going to hurt him, he's going to scream again, but we have to get him up." She leant over her father. "Can you try again, Dad?"

Jack beckoned her closer. "Roll me over, on my good side," he wheezed. "I can get up on my hands and knees. Might be better. Don't stop."

It was the hardest thing Dusty had ever done, forcing such pain on her father. His hoarse cries sounded so pitiful that Stewie screamed at them to stop, raining his fists on Dusty's back and wrenching at her coat. When finally they got Jack on his hands and knees, Dusty turned and shoved her brother hard, so he fell into the snow.

"Stop it, you little baby!" She shouted at him, letting rip her worry and frustration. "We have to do this! We have to get him inside! What do you want to do? Leave him here all night?" She kicked at the snow. "Come and help us get him up."

Jade felt sorry for the kid, but she knew what Dusty meant. There was no point sooking.

"Come and help me on this side, Stewie."

They had to inch Jack to his feet, relentlessly pushing him against the pain that overwhelmed him every time his ribs moved.

"Come on, Dad,", Dusty talked to him all the time. "You're nearly there, nearly straight."

Finally he was standing, grey as a ghost, but standing. He breathed hard, like an old man, and Dusty saw a dribble of blood at the corner of his mouth. She wiped it away before Stewie could see.

He walked very slowly to the hut, moving like a blind man. Dusty and Jade shepherded him, supporting his arms, talking to him all the time, ready to catch him if he passed out. Stewie went ahead, sliding his feet through the snow to check for anything that could trip his father.

❧

Dusty pushed open the door with her leg and stepped into the hut, her arms aching from the weight of the logs she was carrying. She had fed and watered the horses and now she wanted to get the fire blazing and warm up the hut. They had piled all their sleeping-bags on Jack, but he couldn't stop shivering. Stewie had rubbed his hands and feet for an hour after they got him into bed; he wouldn't leave his father's side. She glanced at the bunk, expecting Stewie to be there, but it was Jade kneeling by the bed. Stewie was beside the fireplace, hunched up in his oilskin coat like a little brown bat. He looked inconsolable.

"What's up, Stew?" Dusty rolled the logs gently on to the hearth. Any loud noise caused Jack to wince in pain.

Stewie buried his face in his arms. Stringer, leaning against his knees, looked up mournfully through his hairy eyebrows.

Dusty squatted beside her little brother. "He's going to

157

be all right, Stew. He is, really, we just have to keep him warm." Dusty didn't know if this was true, but she had to believe it.

Jade knelt beside her. "That's not why he's crying." She lowered her voice. "Your dad just told him to get out of his sight. He said it was *his* fault, that if he'd tied the dog up properly it would never have happened."

Dusty dropped her head into her hands. Why did he always have to blame someone? She remembered Rita complaining about it. "His dad did it too. They're a family of blamers. It's always somebody's fault. Somebody else's."

She pulled Stewie's hands away from his face. "It wasn't your fault, Stew. Don't you take the blame for this. You've done nothing wrong." She looked across at the bunk and raised her voice. "I'm the one who made the mistake. When I took Spike's paw out of his collar yesterday I didn't buckle it up tight enough. That's how he got off today, he just slipped his collar." Dusty stood up and took a deep breath. She felt a hundred years old.

"Stew, Dusty, come over here. You too, Jade." Jack's whisper was urgent. They clumped across the uneven floor and stood at the end of the bunk, looking down at him like gunfighters at a grave. "Look, I'm sorry, son. I had no right to speak to you like that." He closed his eyes briefly. "I just feel so damned useless," he whispered.

Dusty crossed her arms and poked the toe of her boot at a hole in the floor. She was wild that her father could be so petty when, really, he was lucky to be alive. Now he was expecting to put everything right with a speech.

"I know what you're thinking, Dusty." He lifted his

hand and let it fall back on the bed. "But don't be angry. You kids did a wonderful job getting me out of that yard. I know grown men who wouldn't have got in with that cow. I owe you my life."

Dusty snorted and began to play an imaginary violin. "Take it easy, Dad, you'll have us in tears."

He smiled ruefully and Stew sat on the end of the bunk and felt for his feet again.

"You've got to stop being so hard on everyone, though." Dusty wasn't going to let him off that lightly. "Especially Stewie. What Barney says is right. Shit happens."

Jack held his hand out weakly, as if to say "I surrender," and when Dusty shook it he smiled through his pain.

21
Making Plans

Dusty stood back and regarded the supplies on the table. "Not much, is there? We might have to eat a cow after all, Stewie." She and Jade had gone through the saddlebags and cupboard and put all the food they could find on the table. "I'd like to bash that roan cow to death with a hammer."

Stewie pushed the noodle packets into a pile. "We could eat *her*. Didn't they used to eat their enemies in the olden days?"

Jade held a silver can towards the light and tried to read the use-by date.

"Some smartypants peeled all the labels off the cans in the cupboard last year." Dusty squinted at the bottom of a can, too, trying to read the tiny writing there. "It's going to be a lucky dip."

∿

Jack didn't eat any baked beans, he didn't feel like food at all, he said, but Dusty insisted that he took in plenty of fluids. She and Jade made him tea and coffee and watery soup, and saw that he drank them. Once he choked on his soup and the pain of coughing turned him grey. He had taken two strong pain-killing tablets when they got back to the hut, and after trying several positions found that lying back, propped up on blankets and pillows, gave him a degree of comfort. Dusty cleaned up his cuts with antiseptic from Mum's first aid kit and pressed a plastic bag of snow against his eye from time to time.

"How come you know all this first aid stuff?" Jade asked her, and Dusty laughed. It was because of the showjumping. She'd sat in the front of the truck on so many hot summer afternoons, waiting to ride, or waiting to go home, and the only book that was always in the glove box was Mum's first aid manual. She'd read it all: mouth to mouth, heart massage, the blue-ringed octopus, snake bite, electrocution. "If I had my pilot's licence I could be a flying doctor."

Jade laughed and Jack moaned. Any movement of his chest was agony.

Dusty looked at the half-empty bottle of olive oil, a picture of a matador on the label. "How come you knew the bullfighter bit? I thought you were a town girl?"

Jade took the bottle and turned it to see the label. "I don't know anything about bullfighters. I've seen the clowns at the rodeo, though. When Mum's had a stall there, I've watched them. Never thought I'd do it myself."

"What are we gunna do, Dusty?" Stewie was still sitting beside Jack, even though he had finally stopped shivering.

Dusty clomped across to the bunk. "We need to talk about it, Dad. What do you think we should do? We have to get help."

Jade sat beside the bunk, too, and the three of them listened as Jack wheezed out his thoughts. He had a hard time trying to think logically as the waves of pain washed over him, and his brain felt like mud, but he'd worked it out. Firstly, Rita would be trying to telephone them at The Plains tonight, and she'd raise the alarm if they weren't there. But the snow might well have brought the phone lines down, which often happened, and if that was the case she would not be alarmed. The outside world probably had no idea how much snow had fallen since last night.

Secondly, Jade's brother would surely have told someone by now that his sister had been abandoned on the high plains, and there would be a search party out for her, but they couldn't count on that. Perhaps the hunters hadn't got off the plains last night—they could be snowed in somewhere, too. The reality was, they couldn't rely on someone coming to rescue them.

"You girls are going to have to ride out," he wheezed. "Ride out along the river. I don't think I can stay here and wait for someone to find us. I think my lungs will pack it in if I don't get to hospital in the next couple of days."

Stewie started to speak but Jack raised his hand. "I need you to look after me, son. I can't stay here on me Pat Malone."

Dusty looked doubtful. She'd never ridden out that way, and the track would be hard to follow under snow.

"You can do it. After you get off the spur you just have to keep the river on your left and the mountains on your right until you come to Price's Plain. You can't miss it because of that big old pine tree. Been there since the gold rush. It's huge. That's where you cross the river, unless it's up too high. Once you're over the river, the forestry track goes straight up to Smokey Plain, and you can raise the alarm at the pub. The brumbies use that track all the time."

"The Snow Pony should know the way then. She's been here before." Dusty smiled at the thought of her horse leading them to safety.

"No," Jack wheezed. "You take Drover. If you run into brumbies she might go wild." His face was ashen again and Dusty didn't want to upset him with an argument, but there was no way she was going to ride Drover. The Snow Pony was *her* horse, and she was taking her. She just wouldn't tell him. Anyway, if Stewie did have to ride for help, he'd be much better off on Drover. The Snow Pony would dump him in a flash.

Jade put her hand up. "What about me? I can't even ride. Shouldn't I stay here with you?"

Jack shook his head slightly. The truth was, it made more sense for Stewie to ride out with Dusty, but he wanted his son to stay. He wanted family to be with him, someone he loved, when he felt so wretched.

"You can do anything, I reckon, after last night's effort." He winked at her with his good eye. "You'll take Captain, you'll be right on him. He'll be handy if you have to bash through deep snow."

They sat with him for another hour, questioning, discussing, planning. They decided to let the cows out of the yard in the morning. It hadn't rained, as Jack hoped it would, so the cows would never get through the deep snowdrifts further up on the high plains. The best chance for them was to go back down the spur. Cattle had wintered down there before, and if this was a false start to winter, they could come back and muster them again.

"Half the cows are still out there anyway," Dusty said. "I hope they're okay."

Later, Dusty and Jade sat at the table sorting out the food. They were only taking food for tomorrow; they wouldn't be spending a night outside. If they couldn't cross the river, Jack instructed them, they were to turn around and come back.

Dusty wanted to make sure she left Stewie and Jack plenty of supplies. "Come here, Stew, and tell me how you're going to cook this stuff." She held up a bag of rice. "What would you do with this?" Before Stewie had a chance to answer Jack banged his tin cup urgently against the side of the bunk.

"I've just realised—you'll have to take their shoes off. Captain and Drover's shoes. If you leave them on, the snow will ball up under their hooves in big icy lumps. You'll have to take them off, but wait until morning; it'll be too hard to see what you're doing now."

Well, thought Dusty, that's another good reason to take the Snow Pony. She didn't have any shoes to take off.

∾

Dusty and Stewie had been up since dawn, removing Captain's shoes. She'd watched the farrier do it a hundred times, holding the horse and chatting as he whipped them off in easy expert movements, and now she was glad she had. She hammered the buffer against the front of Captain's near side front hoof, knocking the ends off the nails so she could pull the shoe off. She was bent over in the pigeon-toed stance of a farrier, facing away from the horse, holding his enormous feathered hoof between her knees.

"He's leaning on me," she puffed, red in the face. "He thinks he's funny." She released his hoof, which thudded to the ground, then took some deep breaths and massaged the small of her back. "It kills your back. I don't know how Ron does ten horses a day."

She picked up his hoof again, this time facing his hindquarters so she could hold his hoof between her knees and work on the bottom of it. Stewie passed her the hoof cutters and she closed them around the shoe near the back nail and levered it off carefully, shifting the tool around the shoe to make sure it came off cleanly without breaking the hoof. She wiggled the nails out, stowed them carefully in her pocket and hung the shoe on the fence. "One down, three to go. I'm glad the Snow Pony doesn't wear shoes."

Stewie laughed. "She's a feral. She is. She's just like those feral people we saw at the Bankstown Show, the rainbow tribe. Her mane goes into dreads real easy, she doesn't wear shoes, she's a bit weird . . ."

"Shut up, Stew, and make this smarty stand up so he doesn't lean on me. I reckon he was resting one of his back legs before. Give him a good whack if he goes to do it again."

She thought about what Stewie had said as she hammered at the nail ends, trying to prise them up, her hands clumsy in their gloves. The Snow Pony was a bit feral, but that's what Dusty loved about her. She was brilliant to ride, but you never felt you had complete control over her. There was part of her that would always be wild. Her hooves were as hard as iron and, although Rita and Dusty had taught her to have her feet picked up, the farrier, Ron, had told them it would be a waste of money for her to be shod.

Drover whinnied anxiously as they led Captain and the Snow Pony out of the stable. "Stop sooking," Dusty said to him, trying to sound braver and more in control than she felt. "You don't like them much anyway." Her heart was racing. She hadn't told her father that she was taking the Snow Pony and she wasn't going to. She just *knew* she was doing the right thing. Anyway, Jack wasn't thinking straight, because if he was he'd have realised that the Snow Pony would go crazy when Captain left. She just hoped that her faith in the Snow Pony would be justified; that she would get them out.

22
Riding for Help

It had stopped snowing but a fine mist hung over the hut, making everything ghostly. The saddlebags were stuffed with their supplies: matches, newspaper, and a bundle of twigs tied in a plastic bag so they'd stay dry no matter how wet it got. They also had a space blanket, their food, spare socks, and a map that Jack had drawn on a piece of cardboard last night, grunting with the effort. Dusty handed the horses' reins to Jade and ducked back inside the hut.

"We'll be off then, Dad." She looked down at him, lying so pale on the bed.

"Good luck." He patted her leg and smiled wanly. "You'll be right, I know, but please be careful. Don't try and cross that river if you can't see the big rock. If the water is high enough to cover it, you'll be swept away for sure. Just turn around and come back. Someone will come and find us."

Dusty bent over the bunk and kissed his stubbled cheek. "We'll be right, Dad. We'll come back if we have to, but at least we'll get the cattle down to the bottom plain so they can have a feed."

Jack squeezed her hand. "Make sure you send someone in with the chopper to ride Drover out."

Dusty looked into his eyes. "You know I'm taking the Snow Pony, don't you? How did you know that?"

He smiled wanly. "I could hear you talking when you were taking Captain's shoes off."

Dusty started to explain but he waved his hand to stop her. "No, you do it your way. You've done all right so far. Just hang on to her if you get near any wild horses. Anyway, if you leave Drover here, Stew's got a way to get out if you come to grief, God forbid." He squeezed Dusty's hand again. "But don't forget to send someone in with the chopper. They can take the dogs, too," he added. "They won't want them in the helicopter."

Stewie was hovering at her shoulder, trying to get her attention.

"What?" Dusty snapped, then felt terrible when she saw the hurt on his face. Of course he was worried. Sometimes she forgot how young he was. "I'm sorry, Stewie, what is it?"

He looked as if he had the weight of the whole world on his shoulders. "When do you think you'll be back?"

Dusty looked at Jack as she replied, waiting for him to contradict her. "If we can't cross the river, we'll be back today." Jack nodded. "But if we do get over, there probably won't be anyone here until tomorrow, that's Saturday, I think. By the time we get to Smokey Plain this afternoon it'll be too late to organise a helicopter and they wouldn't come in at night, would they, Dad?" Jack shook his head. "So," she pulled him close in a quick hug, "let's hope you don't see us back today."

168

Stewie held on and whispered in her ear. "I'm scared. What if he gets really crook? What if no one comes back?"

Dusty held her little brother at an arm's length and looked into his worried eyes, as big as saucers. "I'm scared too, mate, but it will be okay, trust me. You'll be right here with Dad. You'll be as snug as bugs, and you've got Drover and the dogs to look after as well. You'll be so busy you won't have time to worry." She began to walk to the door. "And I'll be fine. My horse belongs here and she knows this country. Just have faith."

∿

Dusty and Jade rode to and fro across the clearing, using the horses to make a path in the snow from the yards to the track leading to the bottom plain. Captain was a terrific snow-clearing horse, he barged straight through the drifts, and the Snow Pony was willing too, though she didn't have Captain's bulk.

"Okay, let 'em out." Dusty waved to her brother, perched on the fence, and turned the horses towards the track. She twisted in the saddle to watch as the cattle spilled out of the yard.

Stewie moved back along the fence and climbed to the top, in case the crazy cow spotted him, but she was intent on moving with the mob, following Dusty and Jade towards the trees. Some of the older cows plunged into the snow at first, but eventually all of them followed the gutter the horses had formed. They walked along in pairs, breath fogging into the mist, happy to be going back to the sheltered valley they hadn't wanted to leave before. As they descended the ridge, Dusty saw Stewie chase the last cow over the clearing.

"You've got them all!" His shout came down to them faintly through the mist, then the hut was out of sight and Dusty and Jade rode on through the snow, leading the cattle down to shelter.

If she had a horse like Captain, thought Jade, she'd ride him every day. When she'd woken up this morning she'd felt so nervous about the day ahead that she nearly vomited, but the big horse had made it easy for her. It was as though he could read her mind. If she thought about stopping, he stopped. If she thought about changing direction, he did.

"It's because you're not interfering with him," Dusty said. "Most beginners yank on the reins and try to boss the horse around, but you're just sitting there, letting him be, and he can pick up your body language. You're a natural, Jade."

Through the snow-laden trees, the bottom plain looked like the top of a Christmas cake—white and flat. The cows began to bellow as they wound down through the trees. Dusty and Jade set the horses to one side of the track and watched the mob fan out over the plain. The snow wasn't as deep here, so the cows moved freely, grabbing mouthfuls of long grass and heath as they went.

"Look, Jade," Dusty pointed. "They're digging." Some of the older cows were pawing at the snow, clearing it to expose the grass below. The girls shared a muesli bar as the cattle settled on the plain.

"Well, that's stage one." Dusty pulled her gloves back on. It was still freezing. "Are you okay?"

"Yep." Jade smiled at her. "That was easy."

Good, thought Dusty, because that *was* the easy bit.

above the track, slipping and sliding on the steep grade—by-passing a fifty-metre stretch which Dusty guessed must have collapsed into the river.

For a while the path descended smoothly, uninterrupted by fallen trees or landslides, and they rode, silent as ghosts, passing through the snowflakes that spun down from the trees.

"It's like we're in a movie, don't you think?"

Jade's fair skin and blue eyes looked almost transparent under the dark brown of Stewie's hat.

"You look fantastic. The woman from Snowy River!"

Jade tried to smile. The valley was like a beautiful black-and-white photograph, and if she wasn't so scared she *could* imagine it was a movie. There was a scene in a film she had seen last year where a native American tribe was riding through the snow, just like they were now, but that hadn't been on a skinny little track above a ravine. At least the track was getting closer to the river now, so it wouldn't be so far to fall.

She took some deep breaths, hung on to a handful of Captain's mane, watched Dusty's back, and kept singing. Sometimes she sang under her breath and sometimes she and Dusty sang together, belting out songs from the radio that seemed so out of place, so urban, in this hidden valley. They knew the first few lines of lots of songs, but all the words to nearly none, so usually they ended up singing "na na na." She wished Stringer was with them, loping along with his sad hairy face, but Dusty's dad thought he might have trouble crossing the river, so he'd been left at the hut.

Dusty pushed up the sleeve of her oilskin coat and

looked at her watch. Her stomach had been growling for about half an hour and it was right. Lunch-time.

"It's a quarter to two," she yelled to Jade, "we should have got to the big pine tree by now. Are you hungry?"

Jade had to think about it. She'd been so scared of Captain slipping down the gorge that food hadn't crossed her mind, but she *was* hungry, she was starving.

"I could eat a horse," she shouted back to Dusty. "Ha, ha—"

Her laughter was cut short by a ringing neigh from the Snow Pony. The mare had stopped in her tracks, head high and ears forward. She neighed again, a shrill trumpeting that echoed back across the river, and began to dance and fidget. Dusty struggled to control her. Captain's head was high and staring forward, too, ears straining.

As the echo died away, a whinny came faintly to them from further downstream, then another, followed by a fierce ringing neigh.

"Brumbies!"

23

The Call of the Wild

"There must be brumbies ahead, down by the river." Dusty felt a sudden rush of fear. What would the Snow Pony do? Maybe the call of the wild was going to be too strong. Would she run with the brumbies?

"Whoa, girl." Dusty tried to rein her in, but the Snow Pony paid no attention. She broke into a prancing trot, calling to the horses downstream as she went. Now she was moving urgently, slipping and stumbling on the narrow path. Dusty could hear Captain doing the same, crashing about like an elephant.

"Dusty! Slow down!" Jade's voice was terrified. "I'm going to fall off!"

The horses scrambled through a tangle of snow and branches where a tree had fallen over the path, then tore up a steep incline that ran away from the river. Even though she felt terrifyingly out of control, Jade was so relieved to get away from that scary place that she whooped aloud as they thundered through the snow.

At the top, the Snow Pony stopped so suddenly that Captain cannoned into her, nearly knocking Dusty out of the saddle. In front of them the track fell sharply down to a small plain, and there, under the pine tree Jack had told them about, was a mob of brumbies. They stared up, trembling and poised to run. The Snow Pony whinnied again, shattering the silence, and two of the mares wheeled away from the mob.

"Oh, they're going . . ." Dusty started to say, as they galloped towards the river, sending the snow flying, but they baulked and raced back to the other horses. She realised that the brumbies *couldn't* run away. She and Jade were blocking the path and the only other way out was over the river. A steep cliff circled the back of the clearing, yarding the brumbies as surely as a set of stock-yards.

Dusty tried to count them as the Snow Pony jiggled and pranced beneath her. There were five mares—bays, a brown, and a grey—and three half-grown foals. And there was a handsome white stallion. He was half hidden by the branches of the pine tree, but suddenly he ran forward, chasing one of the mares back to the mob. Dusty gasped, and Jade saw it too.

"He's the same as the Snow Pony!"

He was the same—an older, heavier version of Dusty's horse. His grey had faded to white, but he still had the dark mane and tail of the Snow Pony, and the same fierce beauty. The Snow Pony whinnied again and it sounded like a scream echoing back from the cliffs.

"Whoa, girl." Dusty tried to calm her, but the mare reared on her hind legs, teetering above the drop. Dusty threw her reins away and grabbed a handful of mane so she wouldn't pull the Snow Pony over backwards. Time seemed to stop. The flat below looked a long way down.

Suddenly the Snow Pony dropped back to all fours, but before Dusty could gather the reins, she launched herself off the edge of the track. It felt to Dusty as though she sprang into space, flying down the slope in one giant leap until they hit the snow, then sliding and slipping downwards, suicidally fast and out of control. Dusty jammed her boots in the stirrups and braced herself for the fall she was sure would come. The ground lurched sickeningly towards her once, and then again, and it seemed as if her heart was in her throat, but somehow, miraculously, the Snow Pony stayed on her feet, and they were at the bottom, galloping towards the brumbies.

Dusty fought to pull the mare up, looking back at the same time to see where Jade was. There was no way she'd have stayed on if Captain had followed the Snow Pony. She was right. Captain was thundering after her and Jade was a crumpled figure half way down the slope.

"Whooaa!" She screamed at the Snow Pony, jerking the reins viciously. "Listen to me, you crazy horse. Whooaa!"

The mare faltered, and Dusty thought she had her under control, that she was listening to her . . . but suddenly the stallion was there, ears flattened, his head low, weaving like a snake about to strike, rushing at the Snow Pony, trying to drive her to his mares.

Dusty threw her arms in the air and shouted at him in her deepest voice. "Yaarrrr! Get out of it!" The stallion swerved away for an instant and when he saw Captain he raced at him like a dervish, yellow teeth bared, his dark mane whipping through the white. Captain turned to kick at him but he was too slow. The stallion raked his teeth viciously across the big horse's rump, then kept attacking

179

him, trying to drive him away. Captain was much bigger, but the intensity and aggression of the stallion overwhelmed him.

"Stand still!" Dusty screamed at the Snow Pony, and this time she listened and stood. Dusty bunched the reins up short in one hand and reached back for her stockwhip, tied to the strap of her saddlebag. Her fingers were too clumsy in the sodden glove, so she cursed and pulled it off with her teeth, then fiddled with the baling-twine knot, sobbing as she watched Captain being mauled by the stallion. It was like seeing a fat schoolboy being beaten up by a karate expert. Suddenly the whip came free. She gripped the handle fiercely, swung the whip above her head and rode the Snow Pony at the stallion, yelling like a banshee. The crack of the whip rang around the cliffs like a gunshot, and stopped him in his tracks. He wheeled away from Captain and raced back to his mares. They were already running.

Dusty chased them, cracking the whip, screaming, driving them towards the river. The first mare propped at the edge, but the stallion rushed at her and she leapt in. Then the other brumbies were in the river, too, swimming for the other side. Dusty let the whip trail in the snow and stood in the stirrups to watch them. She didn't want to panic the foals, but they swam strongly beside their mothers then scrambled, bedraggled and steaming, out on to the snowy bank on the other side. The stallion stood defiantly on the near bank, and for a moment Dusty thought he was going to come after Snow again, but when she cracked the whip he turned and plunged into the dark water.

Dusty kept cracking the whip until the brumbies disappeared around the first bend in the track leading away from the river. Go, she thought, go a long way away so we won't run into you again. She heard the muffled drumming of their hooves for a little while, and then the only noise was the rushing of the river. She flicked the tail of the whip towards her, to loop it up to the handle, and realised her hands were shaking uncontrollably and her chest felt as though every bit of air had been squeezed out of it. As she struggled to breathe, the Snow Pony turned away from the river and whinnied softly, like a normal horse.

Jade was limping across the clearing, leading Captain. She held something up in her hand and waved it like a prize. "I've got your glove, Dusty! I've got your glove!"

Suddenly Dusty's lungs began to work. She laughed hysterically, then she was crying at the same time. She slid down from the Snow Pony's back and stumbled to Jade and they clung to each other as their cries and laughter echoed around the giant pine.

They tethered the horses under the tree and used their plastic bag of kindling to make a campfire. Jade filled the quart pot from the river to boil water for tea and Dusty stood on a log to examine Captain's rump.

"I can't believe this." She ran her hands gently over his big round bottom. "I thought he'd have great chunks of flesh ripped out of him, but the skin isn't even broken. He's got big stripes of teeth marks where the hair's missing, but he's in much better shape than I expected." She climbed down from the log and leant against his flanks. "Poor old boy, getting beaten up by a bushranger." She

181

turned to Jade. "He was wild, wasn't he? A real wild horse. And he had to be Snow's father."

"Do you think she knew he was her father? And did he know the Snow Pony was his daughter?"

"I dunno." Dusty pulled the cheese and biscuits out of the saddlebag. "I don't think horses see it that way. Snow wanted to go with them, that's for sure. It was like sitting on an unbroken horse. She was switched off, not listening to me at all. I think he just wanted her for his mob, and he didn't want Captain. He was a bastard but he was beautiful, wasn't he?"

Jade shook her head as she hung tea bags in the cups. Dusty had horses in her blood. She must have, to admire that terrifying stallion.

They swept the snow off a log and sat on it side by side, sipping scalding black tea and watching the river race by. Dusty started to giggle and Jade nudged her.

"What? What are you laughing at?"

Dusty giggled again. "You," she wheezed, "you holding the glove up, like you'd done something fantastic. After we both nearly got killed, you came out with that! 'Oh I say, Dusty!'" She put on a toffy voice. "'Oh, Dusty! I've found your glove!'" She cupped her hands around the enamel mug then suddenly put it on the ground. "I just remembered!" She felt in her pockets. "I've got a Tim Tam for each of us." They sucked hot tea through the biscuits and made "Mmm mmn" sounds as the biscuit dissolved and the chocolate melted in their mouths.

"I wish we could summon a genie, like in that ad on TV."

"Yeah. We could get him to magic a bridge over the river."

182

Jade stood up and studied the racing water. "Where's that rock your dad was talking about?"

"Exactly." Dusty stepped beside her. "We can't see it, and he said not to cross the river if we couldn't see the rock." Her voice was flat, and Jade felt just as disappointed. They had come too far to turn back now, and the thought of riding on that skinny trail above the river made her feel sick.

"I don't think I can ride back," she said in a small voice.

"You don't have to." Dusty scooped some snow into a ball and threw it at the river. "We're not going back. We're crossing the river."

"But your dad said . . ."

Dusty remembered him, lying on the bunk, giving her instructions, trying to control everything, as always. "Well, he's not here." She flicked the dregs of her tea into the fire. "He's not here and *we* have to decide. I know the rock's not showing, but I think the crossing's changed. Even the foals didn't have any trouble getting across." She pointed at the end of the log they'd been sitting on. "That's been cut with a chainsaw, see. You can get in here in a four-wheel-drive from the other side. People come down here all the time in summer and maybe they've built up the crossing. Dad hasn't been here for ages." She checked her watch. "No, we're crossing that river. Captain probably won't even have to swim."

Dusty made Jade take off her oilskin coat. "They're a bit hard to swim in if you fall off," she explained, as she rolled the coats into a tight bundle. "I'll carry the coats, and you just hang on." She showed Jade how to tuck her feet up to keep them out of the water and undid the buckle on her reins. "Just in case he goes down. You don't want to get tangled up." She caught the anxious expression on Jade's face. "It's not going to happen. We're just taking precautions. Really, Captain's so tall you shouldn't even get wet."

24
Smokey Plain

Jade tried to breathe normally as she watched Dusty ride into the racing black water, tried not to squeeze with her legs, tried to stay calm. Dusty held the coats and saddlebags up high in one hand. She looks like some medieval warrior woman, thought Jade, riding home triumphant, holding the head of her enemy aloft. Captain sidestepped along the bank, unwilling to enter the cold water, but as the Snow Pony moved further away, he leapt in, as Dusty had said he would, and Jade was ready for the jump. Dusty turned in the saddle and screamed above the roar of the river. "Well done! Just let him follow."

The current rushed around Captain's legs and the combination of the water moving and the horse moving made Jade feel giddy, as though she was car sick. She focused on Dusty's back again and saw that she was half kneeling in the saddle, trying to keep her legs out of the water. The Snow Pony's rump dipped suddenly and her movement changed and Jade realised that she was swimming, swinging slightly sideways with the water's flow. She gasped as the freezing water hit her own ankles, so cold it hurt. Captain wasn't swimming, but the water was high up his sides. His hooves slipped on the rocks of the riverbed and he lurched after the Snow Pony like a drunk.

The Snow Pony's action changed again, back to a walk, and suddenly she was rising out of the river, water streaming off her flanks, charging through the shallows and up the bank on the other side. Captain thundered up beside her and Dusty dumped the coats and saddlebags on to the snow and stuck her thumb up at Jade, grinning.

"We did it!" She rubbed her arm. "Oh, that killed my arm and my trousers are soaked, but how good was that? We're nearly there, Jade. Here, hop off and we'll get our coats on."

The horses were steaming, water dripping off their bellies. Dusty strapped the bags back on to the saddles and wriggled into her coat, teeth already chattering with cold. They took turns to do up each other's coats, their frozen fingers fumbling with the press-studs, then pulled their gloves on. Dusty buckled up Captain's reins, legged Jade into the saddle, and swung on to the Snow Pony.

"Let's go," she said. "It's about fifteen kilometres to Smokey Plain, it's a good track, and I'm freezing. If we trot we'll warm up, and we should be there in a couple of hours. Just hang on!"

She turned away from the river and the Snow Pony broke straight into a gallop, fizzing with energy after being in the freezing water. Captain went with her and they raced up the hill, side by side, snow flying behind them like smoke. Jade hung on for grim death until she heard Dusty shouting at her. She looked sideways and Dusty was grinning, and singing, so she joined in with the "Teddy

Bears' Picnic." Then she relaxed and let her body go with the movement of the horse.

After that first gallop up from the river the horses began to blow, so Dusty eased the Snow Pony back to a trot. "I'll show you how to rise to the trot," she called to Jade. "You're bouncing around like a bag of spuds."

Jade grabbed the front of the saddle. This was much harder than cantering.

"Okay, good. Hang on to that so you can balance. Now try to stand up in the stirrups . . . that's right. Just for a little while. Again. Do you feel like he's pushing you back up each time?"

Jade tried to copy the way Dusty rose up and down in time with the Snow Pony's gait.

The snowy white road curved through the bush, misted by the light rain that had started to fall. The brumbies' tracks had turned on to a side track ages ago, leaving the snow ahead of the riders undisturbed. The ground under the horses' hooves was solid and even, and they trotted in a steady rhythm. Now that Jade had the hang of rising to the trot they bowled along, and the exertion of rising had chased the cold out of her body. Her feet were still freezing, and Dusty's were, too.

∽

"We must be getting close." Dusty looked up at the darkening sky and checked her watch again. "We've been going for an hour and a half." They had been climbing steadily and now the snow was getting deeper. As they rounded the bend, the bush opened on to a wide plain that stretched up to the heavily timbered sky line. At first

Dusty thought it was a trick of the light, a reflection of the sunset in the trees, but when she looked again it was still there. A light in a window.

"We're here, Jade!" she whooped. "We made it! That's the pub, up there in the trees."

The hotel faced away from the plain, towards the road. As they drew closer Dusty could see lights burning inside and smoke rising from the chimney. She suddenly felt embarrassed to be racing across the plain. Somehow it felt too dramatic, contrived. "Whooaa." She slowed the Snow Pony to a walk and Captain fell in beside her. They crossed the last stretch of the plain calmly, heads dipped forward against the rain, pushing through the snow like two old drovers riding home from a muster.

"There's someone there, anyway. I've been thinking how awful it would be to get here and find it closed."

As Dusty spoke she felt tears welling in her eyes and saw that Jade was starting to cry, too. She cursed, and Jade looked at her in surprise.

"I don't want to cry. Don't cry. We can't have done everything we've done and then arrive here snivelling."

Jade didn't care if the whole world saw her crying, but Dusty's pride dried up her tears. "You are so like your old man." She smiled at Dusty. "Come on, sister. Let's raise the alarm."

As they passed the back window of the pub they could see figures at the bar gaping at them in disbelief, frozen in the golden indoor light. The carpark beside the ramshackle old building was full of cars.

"Why are so many people here?" Dusty thought aloud. "Whooaa!!"

The Snow Pony leapt like a scalded cat as they came to the front of the pub. There were more cars, four-wheel-drives, lights, crackling radios, people huddled together. The horses baulked at the commotion, and it seemed to Dusty that she and Jade sat watching the scene for ages before anyone noticed them. And then it was someone who'd seen them ride past the bar.

A big red-faced man in a yellow slicker burst out the front door of the pub, looking wildly around for them, the lights bouncing off his glasses.

"Where did you blokes spring from?"

The horses jumped back as he hurried towards them, slipping on the icy road. Suddenly everyone was staring at them. Dusty rode the Snow Pony forward into the light and the man gaped.

"You're not blokes," he said, as though they'd been trying to trick him. "You're a couple of girls." He peered at Jade, further from the light as Captain hung back. "You're the missing girl!"

Suddenly they were surrounded by people, all asking questions. The Snow Pony started to dance and shy and a short man in a uniform stepped forward and shushed the others with a raise of his hand. He was a policeman, Dusty realised, and some of the cars were police four-wheel-drives, too. "Are you Jade Bennet?"

Jade nodded. Then the doors of the hotel flung open and a screaming swirl of purple clothes and flying blonde dreadlocks flew down the steps.

"Jadey!" The crowd parted to let her through and she looked like a bedraggled orchid amongst the dark figures in the rain. Captain snorted in surprise as she raced up to

189

him. "Look at you up there." She was crying and smiling at the same time, and her mascara was all over her face. "Come here, love." She reached up and Jade leant into her arms and let herself be lifted down from the horse.

Dusty watched them hugging and realised how tired and cold and alone she felt. As she thought about her mum she felt a hand on her leg and looked down—into a sea of friendly, familiar faces.

"Hi, Barney, Mr. Jackson . . ." Her voice trailed off and she could feel her throat choking with emotion. "Don't cry," she said to herself. "Don't cry."

25

Sleeping In

Dusty could hear her mother's voice—the lilt, up and down, that made it so distinctive—talking softly, as she did around a young horse. She opened her eyes and looked past the pink blanket to the cracked lino floor, blue with red roses. "Where are we?"

Rita turned to her with a creak of the bed springs. "The Smokey Plain pub, sweetie. I came as soon as they rang and we stayed here last night. You two were too exhausted to go anywhere except bed."

Dusty propped on one elbow and looked around the room, bleary-eyed. She felt as worn out as an old dead tree. Jade was asleep in the other bed and her mum, still in all her purple, was cross-legged on the end of the bed. Rita pulled Dusty towards her and cradled her head in her lap.

"How are you feeling?" She ran her fingers up the back of Dusty's neck, the way she'd always loved. "Many sore spots?"

"Uh huh," Dusty grunted, snuggling into her mother, loving her smell. Suddenly she remembered: "Dad! Have they got him? What time is it?"

"Calm down, everything's all right. You don't have to do any more." Rita patted Dusty's back, rubbing against the tension. "The chopper pilot radioed in about an hour ago, to say he had them on board and was heading for Melbourne. The medico said Jack was okay, but he'd really broken his ribs, not just cracked them. "Flailed" I think was the term he used, and he needed a big hospital."

"Stewie will be enjoying the ride." Dusty smiled, then remembered the dogs. "What about Drover and the dogs?"

"There was about twenty fellas wanting to go." Jeannie's voice was husky. "He must be a popular guy."

Dusty's eyes met Rita's as she nodded. "Yes, he is. Charlie Bell went in the end. He knows the country on this side better than anyone. He should get out this afternoon with the animals. They'll be wet, that's for sure. It hasn't stopped pouring all night and the forecast is for rain and more rain. It might even be the end of the drought."

Jeannie gently pulled the blankets away from Jade's face as she started to stir. "I'm looking forward to meeting our new dog—the deerhound," she said to Rita. "I had to promise Jadey last night that we'd keep him."

Rita laughed. "He sounds like a funny one."

"He's beautiful." Jade croaked without opening her eyes. "He saved my life."

Jeannie draped her lanky frame over Jade. "I've got a surprise for you, Jadey." Jade didn't say anything, she was too tired for games. Jeannie waited, then realised she wasn't going to play. "Dad's coming home. Home for good. He should be here tomorrow."

Jade sat bolt upright. "To live with us?"

"No, baby." Jeannie shook her head. "I can't make it a fairy story for you. But he's going to live in Bankstown, and work at his old job." She flicked her dreadlocks and stretched her arms towards the ceiling, pulling up her tie-dye top as she did, so the tattoo around her belly button was plain to see. Dusty glanced at Rita, watching for her reaction, but she didn't seem to have noticed. "No, we've had a big talk, your father and I. If this isn't a wake-up call, I don't know what is. You and Trav need *two* parents. You need more love and care than you've been getting."

Jade lay back on the pillows with a smile. "We'll be able to go running together. That'll be cool."

Dusty lay back, too, and the girls drifted in and out of sleep as their mothers told each other stories about them when they were little.

"Mum," Jade's voice was muffled by the blankets. "How come you were here when we got here last night?"

"I'm not as slack as you think." Jeannie twisted the silver rings on her fingers. "I didn't worry when I couldn't get through to you on Monday night, but when the phone was still off the hook on Tuesday, I freaked out and got the train back. When you didn't come home that night I rang the Bankstown cops, but they wouldn't take me seriously. Said kids nick off all the time. After Trav got back on Wednesday night with his sorry tale, they got their bums into gear though. Travis was screaming, out of control. Horse was too scared to tell him what had happened until Neville had gone, and when he did, Trav thought you'd be dead. They've charged that scumbag already, picked him up on the highway. And they're still talking to Horse. He's in big trouble."

"I don't ever want to see him again." Jade pulled a face at Jeannie.

"You don't have to, Jadey. He's out of our lives." Jeannie hugged Jade and started to cry. "Oh, baby, you must have been so scared."

"And the Snow Pony, Mum. Where's the Snow Pony?" Dusty couldn't go back to sleep until she had everything sorted out.

"She and Captain are tucked up in the old stables here. Snug as bugs."

Rita started to rub her back again and Dusty nestled into the blankets. It seemed much longer than five days since they had come up to The Plains. It felt as though they had been on an epic journey, one of years, that had forged them into different people. Soon the early snow would melt and they'd come back and muster the cattle again. Mum would have to come, because Dad would still be sore, and maybe Jade would come, too. Dusty drifted to sleep as her daydream rolled over her. The clouds shifted and sunlight suddenly streamed through the window, casting shadows of waving gum leaves on the wall behind Jade's back.

CPSIA information can be obtained at www.ICGtesting.com
Printed in the USA
LVOW06s1046280713

345007LV00001B/43/P

9 780618 771257